DAYDREAMER

...The Whispering Wind

J. C. ANGST

This book is a work of fiction. Names, characters, places and incidents either are products of the author's imagination or are used fictitiously. Any resemblance to actual events or locales or persons, living or dead, is entirely coincidental.

Seven Turns Publishing

ISBN 978-0-6151-9411-0

This is the place where you read what the book is about. I wrote this thing and I can honestly say I have no idea. I notice more every time I read it, and I wrote the damn thing! Here's what I will tell you. There are highs and lows in this book, just like in life. Somewhere in these pages is something for you, whoever you are. No matter how small it may seem, there is a page in this book that you will relate to in some way. It is up to you to find it. There will also be things that you disagree with, and or don't "get". That's ok, that means the book is working. The pages that make no sense to you were written for others. They won't understand the pages that work for you, and you won't understand the pages written for them. Don't get sidetracked by my incorrect grammar, I don't have the time to worry about such things. It's not a requirement to explore the dark corners of your mind in order to understand this book, but it would probably help.

Angst :

an acute but unspecific feeling of anxiety; usually reserved for philosophical anxiety about the world or about personal freedom

- WordNet ® 2.0, © 2003 Princeton University

Forward

This book knocked me out. Its ideas are exciting, the writing strong, well-crafted and at times poetic. It is a surprising book – its insights are explosive and startling. Really unexpected. It's often a funny book too - and passionate.

When you read it, expect to be fully engaged by it. By the absorbing, fascinating and enjoyable conversation it insists on having with you. You probably won't always agree with what it says. I didn't. At times, I was so annoyed by it's ideas that I yelled at the book – but it kept right on going, bringing its flood of challenging ideas with it. When all is said and done, who wants to read a book that agrees with you all the time – there is no fun, no leaning, no entering into mental and emotional territory that really stirs you in that. So, if this book makes your blood boil from time to time, it will challenge and energize you as well. That is a very good bargain.

This book will speak directly to your heart – and your liver and gall bladder. It moves deftly to the deeper places inside you that are seldom visited – it comes to get you there, it gives you strength, and invites you out to take a look around. Wherever you really live is where this book will reach you. What a rare pleasure that is!

Tony Smith, PhD.
Author of *Parzival's Briefcase*

I may not have been touched by God,
but I've snuck a peek or two.

You have never swam the river
You have never much as cared
You who now seek solace
Will find no comfort here

- Chris Robinson

The road is long and windy
Full of twists and turns
But before you can rise from the ashes
You've got to burn baby burn

- ALO

If you don't like my fire, then don't come around.
Cause I'm gonna burn one down.

- Ben Harper

Author's Note

...So here it is. I'm not exactly sure what <u>it</u> is. This book was written over the course of the past 7 years of my life. It is a mixture of riddles, short stories, and various other things. The main things that complicate my mind, fill these pages you are about to read. I don't write in any particular style. There are a few things in here that may not make sense the first time around. You have to be paying attention, I hop around allot. There is an abstract madness to it all. There are many riddles; questions about love, and of course "The Big Question". The main reason for writing this book is to feel, just like any other form of art I guess. If I can make you feel, than I have proof that I am alive. If you read this little book enough times you may even understand some of the riddles inside.

If you have ever questioned the boundaries of the people and things that surround you, you should get a kick out of this book. If you ever question the boundaries and things within yourself, you should be able to relate to what is being said.

Some of the writings inside were caught on my hand-held recorder and written down later. Most were scribbled on various pieces of paper, cardboard, napkins, drywall, pieces of wood, or anything else I had around me at the time. When the thoughts come I try to get them down. They're floating on the breeze. If I don't catch them they just float away. I am neither an optimist, nor a pessimist. Sometimes I act cynically. I can be over indulgent and finicky, just like all of you.

This book is about my journey, the telling of my myth. There are people and things that touch our lives in one way or another. There are paths we choose, and ones that others choose for us. Chances are you will see yourself in here, if you want to look. Ultimately I just put the pen to the paper; it was Art who told me what to write.

...JCA **1-29-06 11:35pm**

You say you want a Revolution
...How about some Instant Karma?

I think you lost the point and now the question doesn't matter. Revolution leads to destruction, no matter how you look at it. Given a large enough time line, any revolution will eventually fail. Becoming jaded at best. Even if it's successful it will leave a disenfranchised, battle scared victory at the end. Eventually the revolutionaries turn into the new leaders and its back to the same game. The rebels turn into the foundation of a new order that always ends up the same.

Evolution on the other hand is completely different. An evolution does not inherently cause destruction. Instead it is an awakening of something that cannot be denied. It is an epiphany that changes everything. An instantaneous shift in mass thinking causing even the most mundane of us to think differently. Evolution is the only solution to the problem (the human condition).

Tragedy and strife are all to often a part of life
If you struggle the quicksand will only take you down
Remain calm and in control, keep a firm grip on your soul
If you're lucky Grace will bring it back around

Curious Cat

Take my word for it buddy
It's best if you don't know
Take my word for it honey
Sit back and enjoy the show

It don't matter who wrote it or where it's from
Everybody gets a shot, so you better run

Make a run for it sister
I'm gonna get 'ya someday
Yeah, make a run for it brother
'Till the light of day

Just remember that there ain't a place you can hide
You peeled yourself an apple and you took it inside
Now you get down on your knees and fold your hands every night
Hoping that your Daddy's gonna make it all right

But there's never anyone home
Just leave your name and time at the tone
We are all on our own
We...are...on...our...own

Tough to teach
Easy to preach
Harder to reach...*Enlightenment*

Every time you survive trouble, it becomes less trouble to survive.

Väinämöinen

This is for everyone, afraid to sail the sea
I'm a fucking Viking
So you can take it from me
Check out the flag on my mast
If you see me coming
Let me pass
You gotta let that river roll
Ride with it to the sea
Hey, you can catch a ride with me
I've been low down my friend
Those who have been there don't talk about it
Well let me shout it
I've been low down my friend!

...I'm not ever going back again

I built the wall
Bricked myself in
Then I shed my skin
You can do the same
Your reflection is to blame
And you alone

Why is a question for children. Who is the question of man.

I just wanna shake it, I don't wanna break it!

Joe Cool

Yes I'm lazy and I'm crazy
The bullshit in this world don't phase me
I'm a lover, and a fighter
I'm a fire under your ass lighter
I'm a shell and I'm a spark
From the ball of light in the dark
Damn right I'm a 'ramblin man
So catch me if you can

Yeah, buddy I got the answer
You got a question for me
If you want it, go for it
Otherwise let it be
Your dream may be a nightmare
Life may just be your dream
Remember on the thin line
Things are never what they seem.

Why buy the cow if you get the milk for free? A finger they tried to point at me. I'm just curious. What does a farmer do with a cow that stops putting out?

Jerkoff

Are you really making a difference? It seems more like masturbation. With your Global Warming, and your save the polar bears. Driving a Prius and drinking a Starbucks. Going on TV to promote your newest all star charity concert. How about the 5 houses you own? What about the fuel to keep them heated? The water to sprinkle all over your pristine landscape you pay so much for? You hypocritical bitches make me sick. If you want to do something, you don't have to tell me. What do you want, a pat on the back? Shut your mouth and count your blessings.

I constantly feel like I'm in a whirlwind, I don't know what to do. I want to go, I want to stay. The nightmare is that I'll lose something either way.

**The Lord works in mysterious ways,
so does the scan button on your radio.**

True Grit

For the hungry ones who can't choke down "because I said so"
The ones who never got an answer, but still asked the question
The ones who beat their fists against the wall,
Convinced that there has to be a thin spot

If you're not a card carrying member

You spend more time digging, than you do cleaning up
For trying to make a point, when they all think you're dull
If giving up is something you watch others do
Pick up your glass, this one's for you

Change...you say you are waiting for the right day

...What if it was yesterday?

If you take freedom to its furthest
point, you become a beast.

They didn't chase me, but I still ran

... Same as the old Boss

We all know *them*, but nobody knows who or what *they* are (are you still with me?). It starts like this, we do what we are asked and don't ask why. Why do you need credit cards when you graduate? "Well it's to build credit". That is where it starts. Allow me to explain. As soon as you start using your card you start to put yourself in debt to the worst bookie of all, *them*. *They* get you locked down and keep you prisoner your whole life. Sure *they* give you nice things... cars, houses, TVs DVDs, etc. All of these things are to make you forget the freedom and honesty of youth that you will chase the rest of your life. Making every citizen into a consumer. With most of us not realizing a difference, or just to broken to care.

Abercromba-go-Fukurself

...Don't trip and fall when you walk in my shoes.

They've got a lot of soul!

Another bitch born with a price tag
It's Ivy League and top shelf for you
Man, all I got is this sinister grin, and these old worn out boots
So until you cash in that trust fund, and give it all to charity
Just clip on your fucking tie and leave the washed out blues to me

Why Not You?

When you were in school and you finished your test, would you wait until someone took their test up first? Would you do the same thing today?

You pull up to a traffic light wanting to make a right turn. The light turns red and you stop. There are two cars in front of you and both are going straight. There is more than enough room to go by the cars on the shoulder and turn right. There is a sign there though, and it reads, "Keep off shoulder". Do you wait until the light changes? Do you wait for someone else behind you to go first? Why do you wait for someone else to go first? Is it safer when somebody else goes first?

When walking with a group of people where do you normally stand? Do you look up to, or resent the people in front of you? Are you happy with your place in that group? Do you blame someone else, because you are not where you want to be?

I just want to rest and say I did my best, but I didn't and neither are you!

Daydreamer

Up on Sunshine Mountain
Past the fields and streams
Through forests full of sunshine
Mushrooms full of dreams

The keeper of time is dreaming
Though he is wide-awake
Where a moment lasts forever
Tomorrow becomes today

He smiled and said, "Come here boy, you have nothing to fear"
I'm an ocean of time child and you are but a tear

He whispered the answer to the question and I began to cry
But I forgot the answer when I opened up my eyes
It must have been a daydream or some old fairy tale
Up there in the hills I hear him calling still

Daydreamer, Daydreamer come outside and play
Daydreamer, Daydreamer you're wide awake today
Just lay down your burden, there's no tomorrows today
Hold the ones you love, and say what you must say

I'm an ocean of time child you are but a tear
I'm an ocean of time child you are but a tear

Out on a Limb

Just a monkey out on a limb
Reliving every sin
In the back of my mind
As I climb, and climb

Working for bananas again
Thinking, is this ever gonna end
As I climb, and climb
In the back of my mind

Everything I wish for, just outside of reach
Everything I want to know, nobody can teach
Always in the back of my mind
As I climb, and climb

One day I will find it
Climbing up a tree
I'll pull myself up on a branch
Where the answer will be waiting for me.
That I hope to find

Always on the back of my mind
As I climb and climb

Thin Air

I thought I had the answer
So I jumped off the cliff
Leaving all the seeds I'd sewn
Just to chase after it

I hope that I'm not crazy
It may be better if I am
Because I gave up everything
In search of...

Thin air is what it was
Thought I could catch it in my hands
It just slipped through
You're right, I don't understand

Try

I am very competitive by nature; I have been my whole life. I don't play for fun. I play to win. If you're just playing for fun, I'll stand on the sidelines and watch.

Still ...
There are no winners in this game
You'll be lucky if you can break even
It's not about winning
You can't win
You can only
Try

Shame on You

I can tell you the secret to the game
No shame

You cheat and lie and give someone else the blame
No shame

Tell her you love her; call her someone else's name
No shame

Sell your soul for your 15 minutes of fame
No shame

Tell him you'll be with him till the end
No shame

He drives up to find a stranger in your bed
No shame

He'll never have the safety of trust again
No shame

Leave them with all the questions and the pain
No shame

Go find someone new it's just a game
No shame.

It's like I know, but I can't realize...

Everybody is not gonna love me.

Everybody is not gonna hate me.

Not everybody is gonna like me.

If everybody did like me, I'd be lying to someone.

What constitutes a friend?

Is it just someone to fill in the empty spots?

Or a trust?

A feeling of camaraderie that can only be gained by spending countless hours and sometimes years in one another's company.

Or a sinister enemy with all the knowledge needed to bring your world crashing down?

...With any luck, you'll never have to ask yourself that question.

Trust...that's what I'm looking for...Anybody know where I can score some?...How much is it?...How much do I need?...How long does it last?...Any negative side affects?

Read the lyrics

Next time you put in your favorite CD. Take off the insert and read the lyrics. Check out what message you are feeding your head. Anyone who is not just a puppet will list his or her lyrics. Check and see if you are listening to the person who wrote it or if they are just eye candy. I like to think of it like I am listening to someone tell me a story, with music in the background. Try it out and let me know.

1 + 1 = 1

I dreamt of the old man
Smoking his pipe by the tree
A witchdoctor captured him
Put him on the outside for me

Sticking out there
Now the whole world can see
Sitting on my shoulder
The old man is ?

Locked in a tree
Nailed to a cross
Cast down from Heaven
Suffered the loss

Gave one eye for vision
Drank water from the well
Reward the brave in Valhalla
Send the weak to?

Hey Tough Guy!

Trust me; you've seen the "tough guy". He's at every concert or sporting event. He's that guy who walks around with a pissed off look on his face. When walking toward a tough guy they will do whatever they can to bump into you. Just to start shit? There like the bully at school, same mentality. I have studied the tough guy and come to some interesting conclusions. The first thing is that they will only bump into you if you are smaller, or you look like a pacifist (in short, someone who will not fight). They will never bump into someone larger, or another tough guy.

I have no problem with someone having a chip on their shoulder. I can get along with anyone who is honest with who they are. Some guys (and girls) are ass kickers. If these tough guys would look for another tough guy in a crowd and bump into each other, it would be fine. The last two times I saw a tough guy coming I bumped into him and said excuse me. They said the same thing back and smiled.

Tough guys aren't bad. They're just bent. Nine out of ten times they were beaten, or picked on when they were kids. So the next time you're at a concert look for the tough guy and bump into him and smile, or just walk up to them and ask what's wrong. "It sounds crazy, but I do shit like that all the time". If you're sincere they'll know it and they'll smile (at least when I do it, there is however a chance you will get your ass kicked) I think that's all they are really looking for. Some people just want to put on a tough mask. **What kind of mask do you wear?**

Chump

I've got to tell you guys about something that makes me fucking crazy. These assholes are out there paying to name a star after someone. I hear it advertised on the radio all the time. Have you heard of this? It's as easy as sending X amount of dollars to the star registry and they name a star after you and put it in some "national book". First off, who gave them control of the stars? If it's your daughter's birthday why would you pay some bloodsucking vampire anything to name a star after her! Just point to a star and tell her it's hers, and name it. It's just a money racket, nobody owns the stars, don't be so simple. I can buy a book and write her name in it, for half the price. Do you really need somebody to create a book and put your daughter's name in it? Put that money in a college fund for her instead. That way she won't grow up to be as big of a sucker as her old man. If there is anybody out there who still wants to send in your money for the naming of a star? Check out this new deal first - from the creators of "big cock" (the guaranteed male enhancement supplement). You can actually own a drop of rain. "That's right folks, your very own drop of rain! Won't your friends be impressed. We offer a 100% guarantee (some restrictions may apply) that your drop of rain will be the first one to hit you every time it rains. You can buy one (While supplies last!) right now for the low cost of..."

Beauty

I have been trying to determine what beauty is. When I say beauty, I am speaking in a purely superficial manner here. Physical beauty. Everyone is attracted to different things, but beauty is universal. It is something that cannot be overlooked or ignored.

This all started a few years ago when my buddy and I went out drinking. An attractive girl entered the bar and he said, "That chick's hot!" I thought she was cute. This led me to wonder what makes a girl Hot, or Sexy, or Cute, or Beautiful? Are there tells to determine what each of these words represents? I can't speak of hot, sexy, or cute right now, but I have some thoughts on beauty.

Keep in mind the fact that this is a running theory...So I go out and I see attractive women on the arms of unattractive men, and it puzzles me. That's not to say that an attractive woman can't be happy with an unattractive guy. If indeed it is true love I'm happy for them both. So let me say there are cases where that happens and it is legitimate. They say love is blind, but beauty is in the eye of the beholder. Remember we are talking about beauty here folks, not love. I don't think I'm going out on a limb here when I say Love is not the main thing keeping the women in question with there "man".

I ask myself what makes them stay with that guy? 9 out of 10 times I fear it is a simple answer...Money. I wonder to myself what these chicks would do if their old man lost all his money. We all know what she would do...she knows, he knows, and we know. My mind races with images and thoughts like...how can she let that fat old man climb on top of her. She is attracted to her physical equal, but her ego tells her she can have 1000 count sheets if she blows the ugly rich guy. Something beautiful would never do that.

The question isn't is it right or wrong, that's not my concern. We must also consider the fact that women can be attracted to a "provider". However, in this day and age of equality, that seems almost pathetic. It makes sense for the other animals, but not humans. I respect most women, just as I respect most men.

I would just like to let women who make that choice fully understand what they are doing. You can get a hot girl, or a sexy girl, but I'm sorry to tell you money can't buy beauty. It is something that is untouchable.

There was a time when beautiful women were taken from their villages by force and given as gifts to princes, soldiers, and Kings. Now they just sell themselves. However, once the deal is made they are no longer beautiful, they are something else. Careful not to confuse angst with anger, I'm not angry. It just seems a shame to waste beauty. Then these chicks get all worked up when there man leaves them for wife 2.0. That was the deal you made honey!

Beauty can be hot, sexy, cute, or any number of other labels, but they can never be beautiful. You can get plastic surgery to make yourself look younger or sexier, but you can never make yourself beautiful. Beauty is a gift. Watching something beautiful cross that line...it just seems cold.

...Have you ever known something was going to happen and wanted to change it? Sometimes you can slow down time. If you are really sincere, you are allowed a moment of grace. That is the closest that you can come, because time stops for nothing. Time has its own agenda, and longs for its journey to end.

ODIN, 3/18/2004

I just found out today that my best friend has cancer. He found a big lump inside his right thigh. We've done so much together over the years but I don't know what to do about this. I tell him he'll be fine and that we'll get through it, but I'm not sure this time. We've been through a lot together since we met six years ago at the Pittsburgh airport. He was moving to Pittsburgh, flying in from Kansas.

I could tell right away that he wasn't that active by his lazy walk. I could also tell that he was very opinionated, just like me. We got along great, my fiancé loved him too, and he became a big part of our family. He's always been very loyal, that's hard to find even in a friend. We would all load up in my truck and visit my parents in Eastern Pa and he was always excited to go. I'm not even sure what his real name is; I've always called him Odin. I've always been into mythology so I named him Odin after the Norse God. Although sometimes I just call him asshole. He's one of those huge burly guys you would see in combat in the gladiator days. So I felt Odin was a cool name for him. It also allowed him to start a new life with us, who knows what his life was like in Kansas; we never really talked about it.

When you spend a lot of time together with someone you really get to know them, you can communicate without talking. This is the kind of relationship that I have with Odin. He'll just look at me a certain way and I know just what he is thinking. I remember the first time we smoked together and he got all confused. Now he just sits there staring at me when I light up, drooling and shit. It's hilarious, he can tell by the smell if it is swag or dank. He will only smoke the good stuff, no swag for this guy. That's what I'm talking about; imagine never paying for anything and then complaining that my shit isn't good enough. But that's just the way he has always been.

I think that if he weren't so stubborn and bullheaded we would have never gotten along so well. He is always happy just to be around, he is a follower for sure (like Sam in Lord of the rings). When he went to get his tattoo, he obviously wanted me to go back with him while he got it. I thought he was gonna wine like a baby, but he didn't say a word. I have some tattoos of my own (that's probably why he got one) and they hurt like hell. I really respect that about him. He's been through a lot. Moving away from his family at an early age to a place he's never been. He had two knee surgeries (they replaced both his knees with metal). He had to take prescription antacid for two years because he was addicted to Mountain Dew. This was right around the time of the "Do the Dew!" campaign. Every time that commercial came on his eyes would light up thinking about it. Yeah we've been to hell and back together. He was there for me when all my other friends turned their backs. When she left, he was always there dealing with my constant playing of sad songs, and late night binges. I realize why he does what he does and how he sees the world around him

I'm taking him to the doctors tonight to get some blood work and setup his surgery. Thankfully the cancer is not in his lymph nodes, so they should be able to cut it all out. With some chemotherapy and help from the man upstairs hopefully he will be with us for a long time to come. I hope that everyone has a friend like Odin at least once in his or her life.

I need an Atlas!

I seem to have gotten lost somewhere along the way. I've taken so many trips; I can't even remember where I've been. That's ok though. I never was good with directions. Every time I leave the house, I get lost. I guess I just don't pay attention to where I'm going. Luckily I always find my way home. For instance, one time we went to see the Allman Brothers in Mansfield Mass. We were driving for hours and hadn't seen a sign. So we pulled over to a gas station for directions. I got out and asked if they had ever heard of Indian Run campground. Now this gas station had seen better days. So had the miserable middle-aged woman that was grimacing at my long hair and tie die t-shirt. She asked me where it was, I said in Mansfield. She looked me dead in the face. "That's in Mass.!" . I asked where we were, and she said Rhode Island. I started laughing and she just looked disgusted. Happily confirming what she was telling me with her eyes all along. I thought that it was great and went out and told my friends. They were not surprised.

Being able to admit to yourself that you don't know everything brings you one step closer to knowing everything!

**We run around in circles watching reruns on TV
Don't ask me my opinion because
I don't like what I see.**

...000 Wake up! Stop procrastinating and pay attention to where it is. Not where fashion or movies are, that's a glorified past being used to calm the generation before us. Maybe they should look where our culture is right now. Everything is just a repeat.

In a world where someone thinks that they can get 10 million dollars for spilling hot coffee on their lap, don't you feel like giving up? Sometimes I do. On top of all of this I'm going to turn 30 soon. I see all these cartoons on TV that are remakes of the same cartoons I watched as a child He-Man, Justice League, Transformers. Am I the only one who realizes they give us this shit so we fall in line? We all have kids now so they give us the same stuff we had, as kids. So we buy it for our kids and in doing so we hide in the past when we were in our own little Eden. When mom and dad took care of us. Then we turn into our parents because it feels safe in that corner. "It's so scary outside lets just stay the same and hope we can get through. It worked for mom and dad".

Just like Chicken Little we run and hide. But what if it already fell? It's pretty ingenious really; just keep rewinding over and over. "Watch out folks here comes the 80's; we used up the 70's"! Stop running; you can't outrun your shadow. The world is a beautiful place, look at it like one big puzzle. Millions of little moments, adding up to a whole. Talk to each other about something more than work or the weather.

Everybody

Everybody listen
Can everybody see?
Everybody wonders
You and me

Everybody's smoking
Everybody's high
Everybody's thinking
We're runnin' out of time

Yeah...it don't matter to me, cause I'm good looking and I'm free
If you like what ya see baby come on in
Chances are you'll never leave again
Over and over and over again...

Everybody's worried, planes falling from the sky
Everybody's thinking, where would Chicken Little hide?
Everybody's thinking it's just a matter of time

I just blew up my TV, cause the news pollutes my brain
Telling us that it's all bad, driving me insane
Little Suzy won her spelling bee but you won't hear about that
You'll hear about her neighbor and how he ran over his cat

Backing out his driveway
It was late one stormy night
Just kick back in your recliner, or you could stand up and fight!

Everybody's watching to see where this will go
Everybody already knows
Everybody's hoping
Everybody tries
Everybody line up, it's quitting time

So when your kids grow up you can lie to them
We'll all dance around the room again
Just like your parents did to you back then
We all dance around the room again

Nobody knows anything,
You have to find out your own answers my friend
Or you could dance and dance around the room again

I warm myself by the fire my friend
Come dance around the fire again with me
La Da Da Da Dee...

Wide Awake

I had a dream that you still loved me
I had a dream that you still cared
I had a dream that you still loved me
I woke up and you weren't there
I tried to sweep her off her feet
But I just tripped and fell

"You gotta do what you can just to keep your love alive. Try not to confuse that with what you do to survive."

- Jackson Brown

"You become a monster, so the monster will not break you, but it's already gone too far they say that if you go in hard you won't get hurt."

- U2

If we don't come to grips with our problems we will inevitably infect everyone else around us with them. Relationships are built on trust, but what if someone you trust betrays you. You see it isn't the betrayal itself that leads to the death of the relationship it is the loss of trust. In losing that trust you will look at the people and things around you differently. You will try to stop this from happening again but it is in vain, a "catch 22" as they say. Sometimes you will catch your betrayer in the act. But the times that will really hurt are the times that you're wrong. We never know, we just do what we must to protect ourselves. To love is easy, to commit is hard, and forever seems out of reach. This is not for lack of trying. You see when we meet someone new in our lives we exchange stories to get to know each other. This makes it exciting, a world of limitless possibilities. You feel like together you can take on the world. Once that high goes away you're left with the flaws and insecurities that also come with that person. If you can look past these, then you love someone. Sometimes you love someone and you can't get past these things. In short, I don't know a thing about love. So I'll just stop now.

Commitment will have you sleeping in a padded cell.

Get It

Here I am. The winter is back again. I'm 31 this time around. It doesn't really feel any different. I can't think of a time in my life I would trade it for. I sometimes miss people and things that are no longer in my life for one reason or another, but not who I was. I like what I am.

So when will I finish this damn book? Why even write a book? Why does a bird in a cage sing? I'm not sure. I'm not even sure who will ever read it. Some of this stuff can be a downer. Life is sometimes that way though. If I didn't put those moments in here, I would be fake. Losing things we love hurts. We all go through it, just thought you would like to know that.

Hearing someone describe where they have been can sometimes help others through similar problems. That being said, I hope your enjoying the book so far. I hope it is making you feel something. I feel crazy right now, sitting on my bedroom floor with a little space heater in front of me writing a book nobody may ever read.

If you are not into the book at all, it's ok. You have my permission to put it down, guilt free. Maybe try reading it later...hours, days, weeks, months, years from now when you may get more out of it. You can use it to start a fire. Keep it in the bathroom, if you run out of toilet paper you can tear out the pages and wipe your ass. I honestly don't care what you do with it. I've kept up my part of the bargain. If you want to wipe your ass with them and say they are the ramblings of a lunatic that is your choice to make. Any excuse you want to use is fine really I don't care. Just remember it is always easier to say that the party sucked, if you didn't get the invitation.

... I was sitting alone in the field when he tapped me on my shoulder. He looked like Jesus Christ, but I knew he was much older ...

WS99 Cave-Tent-House

Blah Blah Blah

The Universe is one big ball of energy. The beginning of the journey is the end. The youngest, is the oldest. There is a source to it all, and we will call that the core. That is where our sparks (soul) originated. The core is a central intelligence and understanding that we all come from and are still very much in, on another level. Imagine an all-knowing ball of electric. For some reason we leave the core to come here and become whatever we are, human, tree, lion, etc. But that connection is still very much there, if you look for it. Our sparks are all from the same pool of energy. This pool of energy is the universe (GOD). For some reason we left the pool and are wandering around here. Separate dimensions, different planets, no matter what your mind can conceive this pool is above it. The sparks are actually like a driver, and our bodies the cars.

The problem is that everyone is too busy pimping up their ride, they forgot it was just supposed to make life easier not become your life. Our bodies are just a way for us to communicate on a controllable level. If we were all in the pool it would just be all knowing, nothing individual. I need that individuality so that is one reason why I stay in this plain (most of the time anyway). If we would collectively come together and except this simple thing that we all know, this world would fall away. But this is a child's fairytale and would be nearly impossible to accomplish.

We need to make simple changes in our lives to make a huge change occur. Bearing this in mind you can call this "core" whatever you want. This is just my way of telling you what I see. If you see it the same but just a little different, "that's fine too"! I'm just trying to find a way to describe something that can't be described. The main things that we agree upon are the things that shape the world around us. We are what we think we are. "Think about it".

You may see a burning bush or burning sky. These are just things to give us a visual picture of something that is nothing. Like calling it God or Satan or whatever. We as human beings have a need to name, that which is unnamable, so that we can go to it or run away whatever the case may be. Unaware that we are always there and we never change, much like a figure eight. Time is infinite and there is a limit to our singular understanding. We would all have to wake up at the exact same time (while writing this I find myself thinking of the song Stairway to Heaven. I'm certain that music is as enigmatic as the bible. You have to listen to the lyrics not just hear them.) That is nearly impossible. We have had so much shit drilled into our heads we don't know what's up. We all had are fingers crossed that something big would happen New years 1999, but nothing did. I guess if we want things to change we will have to make it happen. So we have got to talk to each other and understand we are all programmed, there are more people thinking about it every day.

Step Down

You're out there doing your best in the neon lights
It's love at first sight every Friday night
Yeah, you got all the right moves

Just trying to keep your feet off the ground
Everybody knows you in the clubs downtown
With every passing day, you give a little more away

You say you're looking for love
Do you think you still can?

Remember that time you really fell?
Now you just wanna play show and tell
Are you ever gonna get up?

I see right through you, because I've been there too
Riding on the merry-go-round
If you want your world to just stop spinning
Step off and then step down.

Tongue Tied and Twisted

I'm from nowhere
I had somebody
Who let everybody
Tell her that I was a nobody
That she deserves a somebody

So, somebody left me for something and with nothing
Except for some things we had together
Which apparently meant nothing

Then I thought I found somebody
That turned out to be nothing
Something was missing, taken away

Turning somebody into something
I just couldn't trust
It cost me everything
Which turned out to be nothing

Then I left nowhere where I'm from
To find somebody, to go somewhere with

We will go everywhere together
Until there is nowhere left to go
Then I will take that somebody
Nowhere where I'm from

Which will turn nowhere to somewhere
Because I will have somebody
To go somewhere with

...It should be something

Face to Face

I'm too lazy to say anything
Nobody else is making a sound
The world keeps changing
Nothings changing
Only spinning around and round
Upside down

You'll have to turn and face the face
In your own time, in your own space
When you realize what you already know
Is when you can turn and let it all go
Me, I got a different face
A different time, in a different place

We're all traveling down the line
I guess I'll live this life one more time
Just have to learn to let it all go
It was a dream 'ya know
Just let it all go

Unheard song

I'm trying to dance but I can't get to the floor
So many things out there blocking the door
You know I want to get out and put this show on the road
'Cause if I don't get out of here I'll just grow old
Withering...dreaming...dwindling...gone
Until all that remains is the unheard song

Ship at Sea, 4:15 AM

I woke up in the middle of a dream
Hungry and thirsty a lone ship at sea
Only longing to be free
Drifting and floating aimlessly
Driving hunger inside of me

No more mountains to climb or rivers to cross
I rode them all here and suffered the loss
There are many bridges that I have burned
Many lessons I have learned
There is no turning back

Drifting and floating aimlessly
Only longing to be free
If only I could fly and leave you all here
Stuck on your island year after year

As I'm floating through the sky
I hear a lonely Eagle cry
Only longing to be free
Drifting and floating aimlessly

So I journey out beyond the sun
Where all is nothing and nothing is one
I see a brilliant pinhole of light
Surrounded by the vacuum of night
Only longing to be free

Falling back where I began
Upon this floating ship I stand
A solitary vessel, I'm just a man
Only longing to be free
Drifting and floating aimlessly

Though I am you and you are me.

The Wanderer

We all live in the same house
Life is just a game
If you wanna win it
You have to jump out in it

I got friends in the attic
Some in the basement too
They help me to achieve
That which I choose to

If you don't have your foot on the gas
Kindly step aside and let me pass
I'm screaming, "Get out of my way!"

Because, I'm fully loaded with explosive intentions
Climbing the walls with little apprehension
If they're too big, I'll just walk around

Sometimes I feel like a hand
Without a thumb
Reaching for something
I can't grab a hold of

...A drop of water dances when it hits the frying pan.
Such is the life of a wandering man

Growin' Up

- Smoke, Mirrors, and Lies -

It seems the older you get the less you believe
In all the dreams that seam to slip away
They'll tell you grow up, better learn to play the game
You sit back and watch your goals and dreams begin to fade

They'll erase all your thoughts; fill you full of regret
They're gonna shape you and they'll mold you
Why think it's easier to forget
A cell of insecurity is just what they had planned
Crawl into life a man come out the other side a lamb

Boy you better chase your tail for that money
Boy you're gonna have to work that nine to five
You may not like it but you're in it
You're gonna need that money to survive

I check my paycheck
Where the hell did it all go?
They got all the bases covered don't ask why
Seems like they've thought of everything
It's enough to make you break down and cry

Boy you better chase your tail for that money
Boy you're gonna have to work that nine to five
You may not like it but you're in it
You're gonna need that money to survive

So when you look back on the years gone by
Thinking of all you could have done but didn't try
You just get one shot, don't throw it all away
On their smoke, their mirrors, and their lies

...and Rome Burned

... I was standing in the middle of a field, surrounded by 250,000 strangers in Rome N.Y. at the now infamous Woodstock 99' when it hit me. "Instant Karma"... Even now as I try to write this, there are so many memories that I could never get them all out. I am very impatient and I lose my train of thought. I have many stories of Woodstock; here are some of the highlights:

We got onto the base the day before the shows started (this festival was on an old air force base). I was paranoid that they were going to check our pockets, so I threw my metal pipe in the trash (just a rookie, what can I say). I was figuring I would get a new one inside. " I wasn't about to walk a half-mile back to my truck". Well, as soon as I got through the gate I realized I was in another world. The rules and views of the world I knew where outside these walls. Walking through the gates, a feeling like anything was possible came over me (exhilarating). As I was thinking this I saw this old man with long white hair and a long white beard in a tie die outfit. He really looked like something out of a movie. Of course he would be there! I thought. I realized it would all be here. So anyway, he's yelling out loud, (right behind the guards who let you in) "Mushrooms, Doses". I was like "Holy shit it's the Candy Man!" So I went over and purchased some caps and off I went. Needless to say I threw my bowl out for nothing.

The distance from my truck to our tent spot was at least a mile (I shit you not!). All of the streets were named after songs, or albums (Abbey Road, Crossroads, Shakedown Street, ect.). It was hot, and I had to take two trips (again a rookie) to the truck to bring my stuff. I just got set up when I noticed the people next to me were having trouble with their fancy tent. It turned out they were a couple from Japan. Can you believe that? Just came for the show. Awesome! They had some crazy designed little tent; they were having trouble getting set up. I figured I could build this thing; after all I am a carpenter.

So, I offered to help. I'm a firm believer in looking at directions as a last resort (besides it was written in Japanese). It took us about an hour to put this damn tent up. Then I got them high and we laughed. They could hardly even speak English but we had no problem communicating.

The first night was cool just walking around and checking out all the sights. I got lost for hours and hours trying to find my tent. I have no sense of direction, but this was pathetic. Then I realized the area that my tent was in now looked completely different. People had moved tents in all around me, so I couldn't see it from the road anymore. This was a mammoth festival. Anything you can imagine: Naked people walking around, all kinds of food, a Rave every night, movie theatre, free water (after you have a bottle to put it in).

These riots... They were not started because the water was $6.00. There were water stations set up all over the base. Once you purchased a water bottle you could refill it for free. That was if you didn't bring water with you, if you did than you could just keep refilling it. I don't know why anybody said it was because of water prices and silly shit like that. It was because of us, our generation, we should be ashamed. First night of shows everything was fine, the next night people started being pigs. There was a different crowd out there and they really could not handle the scene, I think it was too much for them. There were some real primitive things going on there at the end.

For me this was a life changing experience. Hell, I crowd surfed over thousands of people and got to the front row. I was up front when Sheryl Crow came on. Listen, I know I was "out there" but I swear she was looking at me and we had a moment. This "moment" consumed the rest of my trip, which was about 8 hours. I was standing on the metal gates up front and this guy was waving me down. (You have to understand that I just crowd surfed over at least 5,000 people. I was in front of about 100,000 plus on a metal rail that is supposed to separate the sea of people from the stage). I was so messed up that I thought he was calling me backstage. Imagine how I felt, I'm like "Holy shit Sheryl Crow wants to talk to me!" She was gonna let me in on all these deep things that she knows (still with me?). Together, that night we could have changed the world. "Ah, but fate dealt us a different hand that night". So I go toward this guy and walk in the direction that he points. As I come out the end of this canvas tunnel I realize that he sent me back out to the field. It took a lifetime to get to the front of the crowd (at least 100,000 people).

Now, normally I would have kicked my own ass at this point. I mean he just wanted me to get down off the gate, and my drunken ass thought Sheryl Crow wanted to see me. ("FUCK"!) But in the state of mind I was in "this was just a mistake". Yeah, it was a mistake I'll just go backstage and talk to her (Listen I know what you're thinking. No matter how messed up I was. This was not stalker shit here. It was innocent and extremely surreal).

So I went up to the backstage gate and got to talking with the security guys at the back stage entrance. After literally hours one of the guys let me backstage. I just broke it down to him like this: How much are you getting paid for this? He said "twelve dollars an hour" or something like that. I said, "to you it's a couple bucks but to me it's a moment in my life". This was a good kid; he knew I wasn't going to mess anything up so he let me back. There are a lot of people who would have looked past what I was saying to him. The easy cop-out would be "If I let you back, I have to let everyone back". That is so weak, no you wouldn't, and I'm not everybody, I'm me. There was a first aid tent set up, and MTV news people walking around. I saw a lot of tractor-trailers, and limousines. I told myself "This is it we did it buddy, anything is possible".

The experience of getting backstage at such a monumental show changed my life. I walked around in back of the stage for about a half hour, and sat down on a stack of plywood to talk with this carpenter. We talked about how they built the stage. I told him how I got backstage and we laughed about the "Sheryl Crow moment". He said, "don't try to talk to any of the artists and you'll be fine". Then he left and I just kept sitting there. I saw Bush walk on stage about 20 feet away from me. From where I was I had a view right past Gavin and into the audience. I took in all the energy from the crowd as they were screaming towards me. It was the biggest high I have ever felt.

I was fully aware that I was in a moment that I will long for the rest of my life. Taking in all that raw energy, the feeling of knowing was very strong. Not too long after Bush went on, some miserable looking guy came up to me and asked if I had a pass. When I said no he kicked me out. I don't know why he cared; I was just sitting there. He could have easily passed me by just like everyone else had for the past hour. But he chose to use his "power" to evict me from the premises. Well I would like to tell him "FU!" and I mean that sincerely.

I personally don't think that there is any one person to blame for the riots. Except, maybe the guy who signed up the acts. If you were at the first Woodstock or any other festival you would know that about 90% of the people there are on some kind of hallucinogen at any given time. So why would you give them insane clown posse, or Limp Bizkit, or Metallica? Listen, I love Metallica, and Limp's all right but this was not the place for them. When everybody in the audience is feeling that way they need someone to "direct" their trip, a conductor so to speak. Since WS99 I have been to plenty of concerts and festivals and never seen anything like that happen. The commercialism of Woodstock drew a different crowd. The festivals that I go to now are not mainstream at all. I like the feel a lot more. When I go to a festival it is to enjoy music, but it is also to get a deeper understanding of the world around me. I didn't like what I saw at WS99, but it is the world we are living in.

Tick-Tock

Time can make you
Time can break you
In the end it's just the blink of an eye

I'm not gonna have the word 'why'
Be the last thing I ever say
I'm changing every day
Still dreaming every night

It's all a state of mind
Our only real enemy is time
He who laughs at all of your feeble alibis

We sure had a good time though,
Didn't we back then
Nursery rhymes and recess
Say your prayers it's time for bed

Then something changed

It's impossible to go back
You can't hit rewind
But you may just get your moment
If you ever really try.

I See You

Longer than a glance

Shorter than a stare

You run your fingers through your hair

I know you're there, I know you're there

It's been one of those days

Where everything is right

The temperature is high, the sun is bright

Reaching in my pocket

I pull out the perfect change

I think I may be happy

It feels a little strange

Should I press my luck?

I'd put my odds at 7 in 10

Nice, she just looked up again

**You could if you would, but you won't.
So you don't.**

Cloning ~ Sweet Pandora

One night I asked him his opinion on cloning. He got that look in his eyes and off he went...

"...Cloning is not the answer...and, and I don't even know why I'm saying this now. Because we're fucked. I mean this is a, this is a you can't go back 'kinda thing. Yeah, this is a we really fucked it up this time 'kinda thing. Because there's no way we're gonna stop doing it. Even though President Bush is trying to stop us from doing it, somebody else is gonna do it. What it's gonna do is become like some horrible fucking cloning movie man. You know how they turn out every fucking time, right; you know how this cloning shit turns out? It's just...'ya know what, why don't we just start mass producing fucking cyborgs? That's what you people want, that's your intelligence level. Do you understand pre-determined destiny? We can only do and say what we experience with our senses. So if they fill your senses with shit to send us in a direction, we will go there without even knowing it. In a sense we are all hypnotized (180 channels). Did you know that one company controls the majority of the radio stations that you listen to, and the venues that the artists play at? That means you see what they want, they point, and we follow. Do you understand what I'm saying to you? Whether you want to or not you will do what they want. Don't cell phones remind you of the stuff in the old star-trek shows? What about styles on TV, fashion, we do what they tell us. We want it all because we saw it in a movie. I saw it in a movie and now my day-to-day life seems empty. I'm going to buy a motorcycle, not any kind but a Harley Davidson. Why? Because in order to be a real rebel you have to pay extra and get a Harley. None of that foreign shit for me, I'm hardcore. After you have it you can talk down on every other manufacturer. The TV told me (and movies too) that you're not free unless you pay $20,000 or more, anything less and you are just a poser. Then of course every thing that I wear will say Harley on it, all the way down to my boxers. I'm just a rebel, not a consumer."

Carolina Crow

So I was sitting in my truck having a cigarette outside a house I was remodeling down south when I noticed a strange thing. I saw a dead squirrel on the road. It was a fresh kill; the blood was still that bright red. I'm guessing it got hit within the hour. Next to the road was a row of pine trees. Within the trees I could see squirrels playing as if nothing happened.

I imagine the unfortunate fellow squashed out on the road was playing with them before his demise. As my mind began to wonder if squirrels feel loss, I noticed a crow landing on the road. It began to nibble on the carcass of the dead squirrel. It had no fear at all, cars would pass by and it would make a leisurely hop to the side of the road until the car passed. This went on for the duration of my cigarette.

Just as I was ready to go inside I noticed some crows in the trees with the remaining squirrels. I think that those Carolina crows have a thing or two figured out. They sit there in the trees and wait for a meal. They know it's only a matter of time before another squirrel gets hit. Do they watch the squirrels playing? Do the squirrels notice the crows eating their friend? I doubt it.

Things can get wild sometimes when you're out and about. Everyone likes to go out drinking with they're friends now and then. Have a few drinks, get a little rowdy and act nuts. Before you do, make sure you look around for crows in the room. A crow will sit and wait for you to make a mistake, and then it feeds on your misfortune. They are a sure sign that there is danger present.

Enemy

Take a look at me
Tell me what you see
Is it an enemy?
They say I'm the enemy

You point your finger at me
You don't know what you see

They try to pass it on down the line
None of you seem to mind
But I'm the enemy
They say I'm the enemy

I see the things that you lock inside
I can bring some peace to your puzzled mind
You try to push it back and put it away
No, not today

Take the book from their bloody hands
How many times until you'll understand
You say I'm the enemy
They call me the enemy

Keep me tucked away
Safely out of sight
Don't ever ask or try to fight
You better keep your lights on at night

Keep an eye out for me
Enemy
That may be just what you need
Enemy...**Are you afraid of you or me?**

Everyone is wasted
- Pick your poison -

All day long the teacher has been up my ass
Kick open the door as I run out of class
I'm gonna pack me a bowl
'Cause I gotta feed my soul
I hope my parents don't know
I'm wasted

Been working all week long
Five, ten-hour days
Just a little sip to clear off the haze
Next thing I know there's an empty bottle on the floor
I'm the only one, who walked in the door
I'm wasted, wasted for sure

You take off your bankers suit, and your fancy bankers smile
'Rollin up that brand new crispy bill
You love to cut it up in single file
Watch it disappear into the mirror (no more fear)
As you feel the drain you forget about your pain
You know you're wasted, wasted again

His plane came in at four, when he got out the door
He was pretty sure that I came through
I had a sun shiny stamp, and I had to taste it
Put it in tinfoil down in my basement
They say, just one drop will do
That's why I take two

Look inside of you
Am I getting through?

Zoloft, Xanax, and Prozac too
They all do the same as the other ones do
If you don't tell on me, I won't tell on you
So swallow down your pill, don't even taste it
You're no different than me
You're just wasted

Ticket to Ride

'Cause we're in mint condition baby
I got your ticket to ride
We're in mint condition honey
Don't you pay them no mind
I know it's crazy out their baby
It'll feel much better inside

I can take you places that you've never been
If she looks as good as... you can bring along your friend
We can shut the door and turn on all the lights
Pull down all the shades and do whatever we like
So won't you hop aboard my train?

Destination no Pain

Just one things for sure
When you walk out that door
You'll be back again
To see your long lost friend
Because it never ends

Hand-off...the marathon

It's ok; don't be sad to see me go
Everyone else has already left
I have lived, and loved
This is your time now
Of course things will be different
They always are
Your number seven
Remember... this cat only gets nine.

..."We're running out of time"

Mountain

Do you look up and stare, do you get angry your not there?
Do you wish and wish yet never move your feet?
Are you angry at that mountain, do you wallow in defeat?

You have to change to climb that mountain
Honey, it won't change for you
You have to change to climb that mountain
Take a look inside of you

You can spend every night wishing upon a star
I fear in the end that won't get you very far
But out there in the distance, a test of sheer will
Something deep inside you wants to go there still

You gotta grit your teeth, you gotta steady that stare
Ignore all of the white noise
It's still there; it's still there

You change to climb that mountain
Climb that mountain you will
Remember every mountain is just an oversized hill

Hell is having an answer when nobody will listen.

What if you could know?

Be careful who you follow my fluffy little four legged friends. There are many Shepherds that lead their flocks astray. Whenever I hear a preacher say, "This is what God wants you to do", I look for the nearest door. The last thing I want to do is be burdened with some fools delusions of grandeur.

There is a difference between a servant of God, and a person who claims to speak for God. It could be the difference between your salvation, and your shame. Only listen to a Minister who says "This is my understanding", or "I think what this passage means is...". Never follow someone who is sure of what he speaks, because no man understands God or his plans. We can merely speculate. That is all we can do. Even a shepherd with good intentions can lead his flock into harms way by making a few wrong turns on the path.

It is a dangerous game, this organization of belief. Trying to claim an understanding of something that may not understand itself. They will say "He is a loving God", or "He is a merciful God". As if there is a structure to God. As if there is a consistency. God can do whatever, whenever he wants. Heads today, tails tomorrow. He can pick favorites, and ignore others. He is not bound by human morality. Who are you to know God? Do you know anyone? Do you know yourself?

Bulletproof Heart

I got a bulletproof heart, and I wear it on my sleeve
I got no time for alibis; I'd prefer you to leave.
I got it all hanging out and I can't put it away
Pages turning, as I'm learning, nighttimes melt into day
They say it's one big stage; I'm out here playing my part
It 'aint easy 'livin life with a bulletproof heart

With gifts I've been given, and some that he took
I can read your mind, just like reading a book

Do you wanna take a look? Do you wanna take a look?

When you dance around the truth, I'll smile and play along for fun
Assured that your not one, not one of my kind.

I got a bulletproof heart and I wear it on my sleeve
I've walked in many shoes and I've lived on many streets
Got a chip on my shoulder that would have broken lesser men
Just trying to get some answers before I reach the end

So I wake up just to greet the sun and play my part 'till my part is done

I got a bulletproof heart
Check it out if you don't believe
It's right where yours should be
It's hanging on my sleeve

What can I say?

I can slide up any mountain
Navigate my way down off any cliff
When I set my sights on something
I very seldom miss

Built a house of glass and watched it shatter
Spent time skipping rocks off the rings of Saturn
Burnt all my bridges and howled with delight
Now they light up my path as I walk through the night

I set out on a journey, one without end
My shadow reached out and I shook its hand
Now, we're a two for one deal; I'd say it's a steal
Maybe I have a twisted point of view

I cashed in my trust, and picked up some faith
Grew my hair long to cover his face
Still, their heads turn my way
I no longer know what to say

I never really did

Ace of Spades

I'm a gambler and a rambler; Every time I catch it I let it go

I don't know, I don't know?

Spend my time climbing mountains, just to see the top

When they give me what I want, I say stop... please stop

8675309 scribbled down in notebooks filling every line

It's all about the journey; nothing's built to last

Wind burnt from the whirlwind,

If you don't know, don't ask ...don't ask

Left you with an empty hole, blame it on that gambling soul

...It takes an instant to create a lifetime, a lifetime to forget.

You can never find your way home

If you get lost in regret

...If you're going to San-Fran-cis-co

- Mercedes every other car (varying ages)
- BMW's too
- 1970's Honda motorcycles everywhere
- Scratches and dents on all of the bumpers
- Make sure the fireplace in the room you paid too much for isn't fake!

I always carry a bandana in my back pocket to blow my nose. I also tie them on my head to keep my hair back while I'm working. I like to leave a little of it hanging out of my back pocket. Maybe I watched too many westerns when I was a kid, but I think it looks cool.

I've come across some information that is vital to any straight guy headed to San Fran. While hanging out with my brother in San Francisco I was told about a "secret code" that is used in the gay community to advertise your likes and dislikes. It's like a secret handshake that only they know about. Apparently different color bandanas in your pocket mean different things. Top or Bottom, anything goes and things like that. I will tell you this. Somebody in the gay community should have told the straight guys about this. Come on guys, didn't you see the potential for disaster with this thing. Honestly when I first heard this I thought we have got to get chicks to do this. It's really a great concept; you go out, see what you're looking for and go for it. No time wasted on somebody who doesn't work. The thing is that some random dude is walking around advertising that anything goes, when he only wanted to have something to blow his nose on because his sinuses suck.

So anyway, if somebody could pass this request for a straight guy color to the creators of this ingenious concept, I would appreciate it. Also if you have any ideas on how we can get women to do this, the straight male community would owe you big time. If you think that "Queer eye" caught some attention, start that colored bandana thing for chicks and every guy in clubs across America will be raising a toast to you.

Crimson Sky

I flew from the west, chasing the sun back home
I opened up the door, I was all alone
Yesterday I had a family, something to call my own

No barking behind the door as my truck pulls in
No more smelling dinner cooking, as I begin
Taking off my boots and shaking off the cold

Now it's all night long, every night that I can
It's watch your back, and keep an eye on all your friends
It's back to the wall and eyes on the door
Light another cigarette off the one you smoke before

I 'gotta stay lean, sharp and cool
'Gotta stick and run 'till I find someone who
Hasn't traded off that shimmer of light in there eyes
Just to fill it all up with empty holes and alibis

I'm in Heaven and Hell here
What can I say?
To be honest with you
I don't know any other way.

Someday...someday

...You run from what you really need.
        Because it brings you to your knees...

It's constant confusion ...Rooftop to the basement...
*One hell of a rollercoaster! ...*You can lose yourself in the whirlwind...

...On my mind

Want it -get it-don't want it anymore
When should you fight for something?
When should you let it go?
Climb a mountain just to piss off the ledge
Jump off and find another mountain

Where is the line between fear and love?
Where is the line between letting go and holding on?
Is it all just killing time?
What's meant to be?
Am I learning or did I forget something?
Beaten down path, or the road less traveled?
Am I broken or strong?

Is Sheryl right, need is love and love is need?
Do I need too much?
Do I want too much?
Get to the greener pasture, winter comes and kills it.
How much longer does Odin have left?
Will I be able to quit cigarettes before cancer gets me?
Will it get me anyway?
How much longer do my parents have left?

When is the next show?
Did I pack my contacts?
Can I pay my bills?

What do I really want to be?
How long will it take?
Will I ever get out?
...and you're bitching that I forgot your middle name?

Hypothesis is a fancy way for smart people to say they're taking a guess. Why can't you?

Black or White
Wrong or Right
Day and Night
Peace or Fight
This and That
Comb or Hat
Jesus or Jehovah
Judgment or Supernova
Love and Hate
Scream or Debate
Luck or Fate
Stay or Fly
Dream or Die
Quit or Try
Go with the flow or Swim upstream.
Don't let someone else determine what You believe.

At the end of the day it's all just killing time. A fact is only that until it is proven otherwise.
Question everything.

The Old Man
SF 10-21-04 8:54 AM

Trapped inside a circle
Running 'round for days
Everything is a blur now
Stuck inside this maze
I see your lips are moving
I can't hear what they say

I'm lost inside

I can sense the beast
Hoofs are clicking close behind
If I can get these wings to work
I may get out alive

I'm trying to touch the sun and not get burned

Walking through the shadows in my head
I found out that light at the end
Of the tunnel is just an old man
With a candle in his hand, cigarette in his mouth
Saying, "Please take off your shoes
Before you enter my house"

You better be careful feeding your head.

The next day you take double the one before.
Walking upstairs you open the refrigerator door.
A light comes on; it sparks something in your head
Bringing life to a memory that was better off dead.

I know you won't shut the door

Everything is changing fast now
What did you see with that third eye?
The pieces are falling together now
Does it make you laugh or cry?

Don't be part of the problem, hypocrite

You wanted some answers you got 'em
Dealing with it, is your problem
Jesus is in a straight jacket, trying to scratch his nose
At the end of a forgotten hallway, where nobody ever goes

I saw you there, you can't hide from me

The shivers go away, so does the pain in your spine
Don't trip and fall, expand your mind
I hope your chute works when you jump off that cliff

If you hit rock bottom, I can give you a lift

The Whispering Wind

I've done it too many times
I won't do it again
Thought I was getting through
But I lost in the end

Just like old women with their knitting club chatter
You've lost the point now the question don't matter
Are you getting the point 'cause you're already there?
Jaws drop open as you sit there and stare

You can't turn your backs away anymore
A drop of a pin, or a scratch on the door
The scream you all feel but nobody hears
Blood red water in a sea of tears

Let's untie the stitch and set it all free
How many of you are coming with me
This time it's different you learn so do I
I will save you from nothing I'm not here to die

Check your coats and leave your illusions at the door
Because I can't stand the bullshit anymore

You will probably cry and there may be some shouts
The room gets scary when the lights go out
Face me you must someday, somewhere
Here I'm your friend but I'm not over there

I'll help you to change that's all I can say
I forgot myself, but I remember today
Remembering is easy, like an old song
I'll hum the tune, you can all sing along

Does this all seem familiar, made to be forgot
Now is the time, this is the spot
It feels like something you should know
But the closer you get the farther it goes

Messages are there but you shrug them away
Just like little puppets up there on a stage
Diversions, diversions, make me forget
You've probably been there but recoiled in regret

I forgive you, but can you do the same
Please! Stop hiding your fears behind my name
You may say I'm crazy and lock me away
That may be true, what can I say

So lock me away behind that door in your mind
Keep me sedated and maybe you'll find
At the end of this road when you call out for me
I may lock you out and throw away the key

It just doesn't add up?

Contrary to what you hear God does not have a house, he's omnipresent. "Seek and ye shall find, Religion is becoming blind. All religions have the answer, everybody claims they speak for God"

If all the answers are in a book, why did he tell us to look?

We were just barbarians, the crusaders changed our minds
With swords and wars and tortures they broke through our lines
We knew many spirits back then; it was our father's way
'Till a bunch of megalomaniacs said, "Let me show you the way!"

Vanity is a sin that all hypocrites share
Remember you did nothing, I saw you there
On that field on that day, when they sent the hammer home
You stood there silent, and you were not alone

Do you think it was forgotten, no I remember that day
Drinking and eating and laughing as he hung on display
Walking through the isles, you can never collect enough
His body isn't bread and his blood 'aint in that cup

It's not enough to be sorry if you would do the same
Taking all of the credit, casting all of the blame
So sleep in his house, lie in his bed, steal his porridge if you like
From where I'm sitting I don't know, how you sleep at night

Yield

The other day I was driving down the road with a friend and he pointed out that someone wanted to merge into my lane. I had noticed this and ignored it. However it got me wondering why? Why had I not let him in? Something about that person made me not care. This led me to question when I do care. What are my requirements?

Then I began thinking about the random stranger. When you're walking down the street, who do you make eye contact with? Even farther, who do you nod to, or say hi to? You may pass a hundred people and only acknowledge one. Why is that? What is the connection? If you think about it there is nothing random about it. In order to make eye contact that person has to also be looking at you. They notice you at the exact same time. Why? Should you say something more than hi? Why didn't they look at the person next to you? Why did you ignore the person next to them? I'll keep working on this and let you know when I figure it out.

Nothing is part of everything

Nothing has to be explained

Everything is

So what's the answer?

It may be nothing

Merlin

Merlin was a magician
Merlin was my dog
He disappeared out of my life
I lost him in the fog

I bent down to wake you
I tried to shake you from your sleep
I felt the chill roll up my spine
The loss began to creep

Deep in my soul out of my mind
The teardrops start to fall
Looking in your purple eyes
There was know one there at all

So I put you in the ground my friend
I guess the place that we all started
Is the place that we all end

Up they're at the corner on top of the hill
Purple violets in an M remind me of you still

Then I built a fire, so high God could see
You'll be coming along there, soon to wait for me

I got you a nice big room
At the end of the longest hall
Where the fire is always burning
The wind is never cold

Do all dogs go to heaven?
I can't say
But if you're not there
When I walk through that door
There's gonna be hell to pay

Last Ride
12-6-04

...Well after 4 surgeries over the past year the cancer finally got Odin. I guess I knew it would eventually. He made it to 7, the age of enlightenment they say. I knew that it would probably happen over the winter. Every winter I lose something substantial in my life. The past three have been the worst.

You get a reality check driving down the turnpike on a foggy December morning when you realize you are about to take your best friend to be killed. That is exactly what I had to do. The only thing on this Earth completely loving and loyal to me, and I killed him. I can think of countless people I would have gladly traded for his life. It was one of the worst days of my life.

By the time I got home from the vets office it was dark. My dad helped me dig for a while, but in the end it was my hole to dig. So I pulled up my truck and put the lights on (it was raining). I pulled my moms car around and shined them on the hole too. So now it's dark everywhere in town except on top of our hill where the headlights are shining on me like a stage. I see a car coming up the drive. It's Vera.

She pulls up in her car and leaves the engine running and the lights on. Now there are three sets of headlights on us both. She starts walking over as I put down the shovel and take off my gloves. We hug each other in the light. After about 10 minutes she said she had to go. So I picked the shovel up, put my gloves back on, and finished burying my friend alone.

What can I do to change it?

I'm only one man

What can I do to change it?

Will they understand?

What can I do to change it?

They make me give in

What can I do to change it?

Don't question, just fall in

What can I do to change it?

Nobody from nowhere

What can I do to change it?

You don't even care

If you subscribe to the idea that anything is possible, Everything is. A thought in your mind is the beginning of a reality. To voice this idea, gives it life. The more people that hear it, the larger it becomes. It is fairly simple to create a different reality in a small group. In order to really make something happen, you have to find a way to inject this idea into the group consciousness. Affect the sum of us. More or less, it's advertising. So, be careful what you listen to, and even more of what you repeat. Because to give voice to something is to make it's grip on reality that much stronger.

Stuck on Red

I know, I know, I know
That the drugs are taking their toll
When I look into the reflection in his eyes

Yes I know, I know, I know
That the drugs are taking their toll
I wonder, does he even realize

I remember looking out the window.
Changing lights, and pouring rain
Waiting for someone to save me.

Nobody came.

That's when I picked it up and put the pen to the page
Releasing something in me that was locked inside a cage

Out here nobody will pick up the phone to answer why.
Nobody wants to hear you cry
You always wanted to be that guy
It's all a terrible lie
They want to own you or throw you away

Yes I know, I know, I know
That the drugs are taking their toll
Riding on this train of consequence

We all live on the edge my friends
So you can jump or you can fall
It doesn't really matter which path you take
One road meets them all.

Maybe you are just looking at this wrong.

A question was once asked, "If a tree falls in a forest and nobody is around to hear it fall, does it make a sound?" My answer is "yes." I've learned to trust nobody and if he said it made a sound, it did.

Don't ask me a question, if you don't want the answer. I find that I am constantly humbled, so I try not to talk shit. So if you want to know something, I will give you my truth. Then it is up to you to decide. The only way that I can break even is to tell the truth. It's not always good. A lot of what I know, I learned the hard way. I would ask you to consider that. Be careful how you judge me. To judge me is to condemn yourself.

Are you awake?
Are You even listening?

Unnamable

It's the handshake and the deal
It's the apple that you peeled
It's that memory you sat on the shelf
That won't go away

It's the glimmer in a new lovers eyes
It's the tears when you say goodbye
It's the vertigo that greets you at the start of everyday

It's summer showing up in the nick of time
Your down to two nickels and can't bum a dime
It's a helping hand from a random kind soul
That picks you up when you're broke down on the road

It's hiding in every corner
It jumps off every peak
There is a name for all these riddles
That name I dare not speak

I hope you find what you're looking for,
...without getting what you're asking for.

Once upon a time ... *in a place that's never far, I was dealing blackjack to Jesus Christ and The Morning Star. One wore black and one wore white. I couldn't tell the difference by the soft candlelight.*

I remember he slammed his fist on the table. I wasn't really listening to what they were saying to each other, up to that point. I was certainly listening now, and trying to catch up on there obvious difference of opinion. "I have better hair – look at it!" The other guy just shook his head. I'm sure he had heard this little rant countless times before. So they turned to me and asked me who I thought was right. I told them both it was their fight. I'm just here to deal the cards.

Multiple Choice
4-15-04 11:20 PM

- Solves all problems
- Takes the pain away
- Brings people together
- Makes life worth living
- Will get you through the tough times
- When it's real, it will consume your life
- Teaches you things about yourself, you never knew
- It's obvious in your eyes
- Shapes our world

a.) *Love*
b.) *Hate*
c.) *Nothing*

77

That Guy

Who's that guy, you ask? It is the guy that gets you in trouble. What kind of trouble you ask? All kinds of trouble, the good kind of trouble, and the bad kind of trouble. I can't speak of your guy, but I can tell you a little bit about mine. If you are listening correctly you may get some hints as to what your guy is up to.

Before I get into this, let me say that I have come to an understanding with that guy. He's not really bad, he's just ??? I don't really know how to describe him. I can say this he is not that complicated, and then again sometimes he is. He is actually fucking with me right now...stopping the words from coming outside to play with all of you.

He likes to be mysterious or some shit like that, and sometimes he is. However he is no mystery to me, I did make him after all. Much like Frankenstein I put him together with bits and pieces of people I have encountered along the way. That's not to say I am responsible for what he has become. Sure I put the pieces together, but it thinks for itself. He wears things and says things that I would never say. He also knows, and notices things I never would.

For instance one time when the radio was scanning in my truck, he reached out and stopped the dial. I knew the song he had stopped it on, it was the song Mr. Jones by the Counting Crows. Now I can tell you this, I would have just let that scan keep on rolling. I'm not really a big fan of the song. I went to hit the scan button again, but he stopped me. So I said "what the fuck dude, this song sucks!". To which he replied "Do you know the difference between listening, and hearing? Because I don't think you do. This song is about Me". I thought to myself...Oh great here we go, it's time for him to climb up on his soapbox.

He told me that the song is about the two sides of a personality, just like us. Then I said, "I thought you said the song is about you"? He answered, "It is, everything is. However it is also about your lame ass". I hate when he says that shit, but was curious to hear what he was talking about. Because although he may at times act a bit crass, the way in which he sees the truth in a thing amazes me.

So I ask him to explain. The following was his word for word response...

"I don't even know why I say anything to you, you're so damn simple. It just seems a waist to see you eat the crumbs they give you, when there is a feast right under your nose. So the song is about this guy at a bar. I think it's the New Amsterdam. He's checking out some blonde girl. Mr. Jones is talking to some wild chick about whatever. Now hears where it can get tricky. He's speaking to you about himself. Himself being comprised of two parts, him and self...like me and you. So he's sitting there with him at the bar like two buddies, ya' know what I mean. There checking out the girls, trying to tell each other some of the girls are checking them out. He likes Bob Dylan, Mr. Jones likes something a little more funky. Your not getting any of this are you? Fuck it! change the channel, the songs over now anyway. Next time you hear it, listen."

I forgot all about it and wrote it off as one of his rants. A few weeks later, the song came up again on scan, so I stopped it and "listened". I'll be a son of a bitch if he wasn't right. It is about the two sides of some dudes personality. So yeah, sometimes he makes sense. Learning to Fly, by Pink Floyd, you should hear his thoughts on that one. So I admit he sees more than me, but I keep this ship afloat. Granted it may look like a wreck, but I assure you it can weather a storm.

So as I explained earlier, he gets in his philosophical moods every now and again. He enjoys creating things and burning things. He is honestly the reason why my fingers are typing right now. He doesn't care that I failed typing class and have to use two fingers to type all this shit. I was happy just relaxing, but he had to write.

Getting back to my original thought, that guy. It is the side of you that is your opposite. Jung calls him the shadow. Honestly you should just put this book down and go get something of Jung's. I have read allot of his stuff, and can relate to what he is saying. However the language needed to really state the truth of a thing, that requires patience. I fall very short in the patience department. Actually, I'm done with this one, I'm all over the place here. To much to say, to long to say it. If we should ever cross paths I'll explain it in more detail. Just remember to keep an eye on that guy.

Divide and conquer...

Every time I turn on the television I get depressed with the world. Flicking through movies, commercials, and the news. You hear about the latest celebrity scandal, a rape or murder in your neighborhood and it makes you scared of the world that we live in. Makes you run home after work and watch TV in the "safety" of your home. That's exactly what they want you to do. Then they can tell you what disease or biochemical weapon to watch out for.

Why is it you think that they tell us all of these things? If the terrorists hit us with a chemical weapon, we are screwed. You won't be able to do anything about it so why make us stress about the horrible effects of some gas that should have never been made to begin with. To break our spirit, that's why. Divide and conquer the oldest trick in the book and still the best!

Example:

Turn on any news channel and you are likely to hear some race baiter saying how it's so unfair for minorities and how the world holds them down. When I hear all of this bitching all the time I ask myself are they talking to me. I really take it personally... "Oh my God he said black instead of Afro-American!"(Yes I did) By the way, I have never come across a black man who was offended at being called black instead of African American. Much in the same way I have never met a white man who gets offended if not referred to as a Caucasian. Although I'm certain people like that exist, they are in the minority (and they are uptight assholes!).

So why is it that these are the only people we see representing us? All that black and white stuff is getting old. They want us to fight. Apparently I am a rare breed of individual, a single, and straight, white, male. Where do I sign up for minority benefits? Do you feel that just because I'm a white male that life is handed to me on a silver platter? Is it fair to me that I can't say anything or I get racist branded into my forehead?

When your bitching about slavery and you were never a slave, and I never owned a slave. It seems like someone who is too lazy to do anything other than bitch and they want to make me their scapegoat. Honestly, if you would practice what you preach, you would move off of the Indians land. I'm sorry about the Indians too, so why don't we ever hear about them? We're all on their land!

The "Instigators" are very busy creating "non-profit minority" organizations as a cover-up for strong arming companies into hiring whom they say. Constantly throwing fresh brush on smoldered ashes. If these companies don't comply with the demands, the race card is dropped and the smearing, and picketing begins. It's sad, they are the same as the racist assholes who said no blacks allowed in the 50's. We are only switching roles, but guess who stays the same? "Meet the new boss, same as the old boss!"

Now there are plenty of organizations, and colleges that only blacks, or other "minorities" can join. If there is a white's only club though, they call it racist. I'm confused. Do these people just like to see themselves on TV? I got enough of my problems to deal with, so stop whining. I'm aware that there are racist assholes out there that think it's cool to pick on black people. They are just like the black racist on TV asking for special treatment. If all the chips are stacked against you, then why are you on TV? Use your head. Life is tough for everyone. They like us to fight, that way we don't ever evolve. Neither the white bigot, nor the black racist does any good for their selective tribe. There are many who enjoy and profit off the struggle on both sides. They are the real problem. It's certainly not my fault. I get along with all different kinds of people, regardless of color.

I'm not on TV complaining about all of the trash from the city being dumped into my back yard. They built a dump right down the road and they truck in the trash from out of state. If it is racist and ass-backwards where you live, move. If the dump gets to be too much for me I will do the same. I'm saying if you got nothing you got nothing to lose. Just move!!!!!!!!!!!!!!! It seems as though the media (propaganda, depending on how you see it) has a vested interest in keeping black and white separate, while saying they want us to be as one. These are old wars and things are getting better for every minority as far as I see. Things may even be getting a little hypocritical if I dare say. Why is there an option for Spanish when you call the phone company or you read directions? Isn't that discrimination? Why not Russian, or German? Why not just English? Why do I have to stand in line at the airport for an hour for safety checks? When there are thousands of people crossing the border illegally every day. For Mexican votes my friends. Who cares if they're a citizen, as long as they're a consumer! I have no problem with someone coming here. Besides, they had the courage to leave all they knew in search of something better. "If you have nothing you have nothing to lose".

However, just as I would expect a guest in my home to respect and follow the laws and customs of my house I expect the same of my homeland. If your house is burning and you want to stay at my house that's fine. Don't come in and change the furniture or paint it a different color to make it feel more like your home. It's my home and I like it the way it is. Be happy that I let you sleep on my couch. I don't think it is too much to ask of you to learn our language. Would you stay at my house and expect me to learn your language? If you come to America learn our language, if I move to your country I will do the same.

"Yeah, it's a funny thing having an English-speaking operator in an American town on an American phone". They like to make you feel like we are being racist or self righteous, but it is nothing like that. Everyone says nothing for fear of being labeled a racist. "While I'm writing this I'm afraid of some race-baiter putting a spin on this and making me seem as though I am a racist". This is not true and I would be glad to debate anyone face to face who feels differently so they know that. It's a very touchy subject and I feel that these things must be said. Nothing being said will only continue to breed resentment on both sides ("don't think for a second that they don't know that!") I'm just trying to say enough is enough. If you want to hear Spanish move to Spain. If you want a chance at a better life in the greatest country in the world, please just show a little appreciation. Here or there, why should you have it all but I can't. "Oh yeah, that's right it's because I'm a white male, the center of everything evil in the world". Well go sell your bullshit somewhere else we're all stocked up here!

Race is just one place where divide and conquer works. They also like to keep different religious institutions at odds with one another. The trick is to make us see the differences we have and ignore the things that we have in common. The main problem that we all share is them. Have you ever seen the painting of the Lion lying with the Lamb? To me this painting is an enigma telling us that we must work together. We all have more in common than you think. You have more in common with your "enemy" then you think. We agree almost all the way home. So lets all hop on the bus and you can get off whenever you like. Come on Guys! The Justice League worked with the Legion of Doom, MacGyver worked with Murdock, and The Duke boys worked with Boss Hog. These are obviously just light-hearted examples, but the concept is simple. We have to come together if we want this shit to go away. That means all sides have to drop the shit from the history books, and start writing our own.

Trust in what you know, but believe there is more.

When they say they hear you
You're on your own
When they say they're with you
You are not alone

Reflections

He looked at his parent's picture letting out a sigh
The ones he thought knew everything
Can't answer his questions why
I guess we all have to face the face
I saw mine at 23
Looking in the mirror
Someone else looked back at me
...And he cried

Empty

You broke her and she broke you
    Did all the things first timers do
Now you're questioning why
    It's what you wanted
Don't lie
    You wanted something
Or was it nothing
    Isn't everything
It never ends
    Only starts again
Until the end
    Let's do it again

Dear Everybody

What to say, what to say? You won't believe it anyway. A truth so wonderful it could change a mind. That's the kind...that's my kind.

Let's just assume for the sake of argument. Is it possible for me to play Devils advocate for just an instant when I tell you that to know a thing can change a thing. What if I were to tell you something? Could that something change anything?

I already know the answer to that question. That's not all that I know either. Because if I know a thing, then you must also know that thing. Because it was you who I learned everything from. It was you who taught me every hard lesson and showed me every kindness without question. It is for all of you that I finally put the pen to page so that I can help you face a thing. In helping you face a thing, I will then be able to face a thing. I am a sum of your parts. What glimmers in you, shines in me.

I only go where I'm wanted and I always leave to soon. I learn something new everyday, and pick up things as I move along. I'm out here and I'm watching, so be good...for goodness sake.

**Keep your head up
Don't look down on your sisters and brothers
If you know yourself you will understand others**

The Piper

...Takes me to a place you may not understand
where I know I'm something more than just a man

When I'm high I want to get low
When I'm low I wanna be high
He shows me things I've never seen
Maybe that's why

Now did I see him or did he see me I'll never understand
When I try to walk away, he comes and grabs me by the hand
If you ever hear him coming better turn and run away
Because once you really listen
Things will never be the same

It's in the way the shadows move
He's why the babies cry
He'll use you up and then move along
Won't even bat an eye

You'll question was he really there?
That's the trick he plays
Don't even look, he's Always
There waiting in the haze

He's the Piper, listen to his words
Hear what he has to say
He'll tell you things you never knew
You'll be amazed in every way

Watch how long you follow him
You may end up alone
Wake up on a picnic bench
That's now become your home

7:10 A.M. Procrastination
12-10-03

When I wake up in the morning, and when I go to bed at night I am filled with regret and shame. It feels as though the sweet has turned to sour. I realize that it is my fault. Procrastination is my name. I have talked shit for so long without doing any of it that I'm afraid that my chance is over. I have wanted to write movies, make music, write a book. These are all dreams of mine. The constant need to connect and the belief that anyone can make a difference. Even You...

Blue Collar Blues

4-5-04 1:30 A.M.

For everybody out there struggling in this economy. Wanting to get a raise, but you can't compete with the little kids on team NAFTA. Try to keep your heads up at those union meetings. Imagine how the gas station attendant is feeling right about now. It was all right before 9-11. Just sit on your ass all day and watch TV. Ever since then I see him out there every day changing those prices. Usually around rush hour (I guess it must cost them more to run the pumps when it's peak drive time!), I see that little guy go out there carefully changing those numbers. I wonder if they are doing any better with a raise? Since there workload has doubled I'm sure there raking in the big bucks. My advice is to look for jobs at a gas station guys. You should have excellent job security. It doesn't seem as though we are going to use any other alternate forms of fuel in the near future. With the gas prices going up you can certainly move up in the service station world.

Yeah, sure they blow sunshine up our ass around election time. They love talking about environmental change, and losing our foreign dependency on oil. Just like they want us to lose our addictions to cigarettes. I find it fascinating that they created this whole "Truth" campaign about cigarettes. They make it look like some trendy indie flick. The real "truth", is that Philip Morris funds those ads. The same company that sells us the cancer sticks in the first place. Think about it? They couldn't possibly want us to stop, they would lose money.

The thing that you have to realize is that it doesn't matter what they do. It's what they let us know they are doing. There are a lot of things like that going on around us right now. All of these big corporations are laughing at us all the way to the bank. They look at us like sheep in the pasture, just good old American "consumers". Have you ever really thought about what that word means. Think about it, the word "consumer". They just fill us up and get us nice and plump like baby veal, licking their chops and getting hungrier everyday. Perfectly content with how the system is working for them. Smug in there assurance that nothing ever changes. Actually we can make a change, but we would have to look past the smoke and mirrors. Stop thinking there is a difference between black and white, or Christian and Jew. There are differences that we share, but they are only skin deep. The real problem is the people out there pushing these fights. Always talking about problems, never solutions. Always showing us how different we are. Showing us that we should watch out for someone different - reminding us of old grudges.

It is easy to get frustrated and wrapped up in the day-to-day madness of our lives. We get swept up and the hours, days, years pass by without any significant changes. Your spirit is smothered by the worries of the day. Will you be able to pay the bills? Can you get your project done on time? Will your kids be ok? No matter who you are, or how many friends you have, you are still on this journey alone. It is only fear that stops you from making the change. It is your spirit, or subconscious that suffers the most.

Running with the pack

We all choose our path. We all walk down Shakedown at some point in our lives. Whether it's a field in Tennessee, Hollywood Blvd., or a side street in Times Square. Most things aren't what they seem. The Devil is on every corner, and Angels are walking by. Nothing is ever missed by the eye in the sky.

Nobody is perfect. Everyone must learn in their own way. Some never learn at all. You determine what you will be by the places you go, and the people that you meet. It's in the music you listen to, the books you read, and the choices that you make. All of these things and so much more blend together to determine the person that you become. Yours is not to judge. Your time is wasted if it is spent throwing stones. I don't ask you to be like me, and I don't want to be you. Try to understand that we are all pieces of a larger whole.

I go places you won't, and tell you of the things I've seen. You do the same for me. This is the only way to make all your dreams come true. Everyone plays his or her part, and everything gets done. Some get married and raise a family, some don't. If you can share with each other and actually empathize with one another you can have it all.

Wasted Words

What would you say if I told you I knew?
Where it all started
Where it leads too

Would you fear me, embrace me
Or deny due to doubt
The scream we all hear
We don't talk about.

I'll never save him
He's gonna save me
Another lamb to the slaughter
So that I may feed

We'll all turn our backs
Bow our heads in shame
We pass it all down
The wisdom and pain

What will we do
Now the lambs run away?
Cry and beg forgiveness
Judgment day

Girl Next Door

So you drew me a picture
I'll write you a little poem
Talking 'bout the good times to come
And the bad ones that have gone

Knew it when I saw the gold
Yellow flashing in your hair
Turned to take a glance
Got caught in a stare
I caught you looking back
A little grin, flick your hair for me

A style and smile that says so much
Without saying a word
Others may have missed it
You can be damn sure that I heard

Want to put you in a bottle
Because I don't like to share
Wanna write this down on paper
So I'll always have you there

The tide is turning
The waves are breaking
There's fire in the sky
The heat is rising
Your eyes are smiling
Standing by my side

So, baby thank you for that picture
I wrote this one for you
Just remember that the past is gone   ...Sadly so are you

Lilith

I saw some scribbled lines on my notebook
Orange made me think of you
Reached and grasped, tried to hold on to the brighter side of

You shut out the light and started spinning
Like you always seem to do
Go ahead put the blame on me
If that makes it easier for you

Be careful spinning around in the darkness
I know the pleasure is in the fright
Remember if you spin around for to long
You may misplace the light

Can you tell me?
What else could I do but walk away?
Try to save my light
To get me through another day

I dreamt of you standing
Naked in the storm
Told you, come sit by the fire
I can keep you warm
If only for a little while

You pulled away or got swept away
Honey, I ain't placing no blame
You take care of yourself now baby
I'll go out the same way I came

Rock Star

- *Without the Fame* -

Why you sittin' here listening to me?
Ain't there somewhere else you outta be?
Why you listening to the words that I say?
I'm gonna change them by the end of the day

Look at me up here I'm so cool
Remember baby I'm just playin' the fool
You wanna know about the things in my mind
I'll crack the door you gotta walk inside

I'll warn ya' honey you won't like what you see
You like the shell but it's not me
Been here before gonna do it again

Kiss me baby, I'm your long lost friend

Pushed me away, I put the pen to the page
Now I just sit back and I sing what he says
It don't sound bad and it's working for me
Rock rollin' down the hills of sanity

I still think about it sometimes
The life that could have been mine
I had to let it go
It was a dream you know
They say I can't ever win
That's why I get up and do it all again

Yeah! Winding your way down to Bakers Street
Lots of people you'd like to meet
Might find some people wish you never knew
Could find out one of them people is you

Pushed me away, I put the pen to the page
Now I just sit back and I sing what he says
It don't sound bad and it's working for me
Rock rollin' down the hills of sanity

Just a rock star without the fame
Nobody left to blame
I'm still here

But you know I still think about it sometimes
The life that could have been mine
I had to let it go
It was a dream, I know

They say I can't ever win
That's why I get up and do it all again...

To whom it May Concern

I read your article last month "The Losing War", and it's comparison between Iraq and Vietnam. I thought about all the people lost in that senseless war. The reason I wrote in was to tell you about my son. There are some wars that are not talked about in history class; my son was in one of them.

The times were tough back then, just like they always are. The age of my son and the war he fought are all but forgotten now. Just another screenplay for some movie executive, or a best seller on the book club. The meaning of any war seems to get lost in the haze, as egos and wallets need to be filled.

My son was right by my side his whole life. I guess that was my fault, but I really loved the boy. I didn't want to see anything happen to him. He was a beautiful young man. You see the thing about being beautiful (I don't mean physical beauty) is that everyone looks up to you. Which at first is a great thing, but when they can't do what you can they want to get rid of you, to lower the bar (if you know what I mean).

They were standing by his side one second, and stabbing him in the back the next. The people he was trying to help were self-imprisoned. They all wanted a change, but no one wanted to take the first step. That's why we went, to give them something substantial to believe in.

This scared their leaders. They said they wanted my son dead. Not for doing anything wrong, but for doing everything right. They claimed he was creating civil unrest among the people. This did not scare my son. In his letters he told me "These people are really coming around, I'm making a big difference here!"

Time went by and more people began to listen to my son. He could get along with anyone. He led by example. He really had an amazing way with people; wish I could say the same. I was watching it everyday, just as you do at home on your TV. War has a way of becoming entertainment, when you see it from above. When you are on the ground fighting for your life it is no game at all.

Their leader offered a reward for my sons capture. They said he was a threat to their power, and must be killed. However my son was very stubborn, and would not back down. Eventually they captured him. He actually allowed himself to be captured. The only way to know if these people were strong enough to make it on their own was to test their loyalty.

Everyone wanted him set free, but no one would stand up. They were all afraid. The sad irony of this is that if one had stood, all would have followed. They all just stood there and watched them torture my son in silence. He died because they were weak.

The good news is that everyone loves a martyr. They still tell stories of what a great man he was, and how he changed the world. When the children ask, "If he was so great, why did he have to die?" All of the adults chime in "For us!" I find that fascinating, he died for them. It's more like he died because of them. Yeah he died for their sins all right. Their sin was to do nothing, the same thing they would all do today. Nothing has changed.

Actually, they did build a statue of him downtown. They make all kinds of money off of him. There are shops that sell T-shirts, books, songs and movies about my son's life. Hell, they even have clubs where they talk about how great he was (you can also get the latest town gossip). The one thing that they don't talk about is blame. They act as though it had to happen, and there is no blame. Tell that to his family.

Well I guess I said enough. There is certainly more I could tell you, but I don't think it would do much good anyhow. My youngest son just got a letter in the mail the other day, asking him to go fight. He said no thank you; I'll just stay right here and take care of myself, just like everyone else. I hope someday I'll be able to pay those bastards back for what they did to my son. I know that isn't very Christian of me, but which one of you would feel any different?

We're all made of stars and we all turn to dust hubba, hubba, hubba, who do 'ya trust?

Judge by what you see
Not what they told you
Or in the end you may get borrowed
Or sold too
The choice is yours alone

There are many different points of view
Some of them pointed at
You simply say I'm a man
He who kills that which he doesn't understand
Or cages it up and throws away the key

The friend of a friend
May be an enemy to you
Or an enemy of he may be liken to
You will understand in due time

Sticks and stones may break your bones
At the end of the line
You walk through alone
The same way you came out
Asking what's this all about

...and who the hell am I?

...But a Dream

I've been to the top of the Dark Tower and it's not empty
Spent some time with Lucy in the sky

I've been climbing on rock bottom
Just watching the wheels of time pass by

Mr. Jones has always been a friend to me
Since I joined the cult of personality

I bought a one-way ticket on a runaway train
I've wasted some time on the dock by the bay

I was under my dreaming tree and singing a song
When I heard the Man in Black was gone

When the Prince of Darkness has a sitcom on TV
Where believing in Jesus has a minimum fee

When all the pieces are there, and don't seem to fit
When the sunshine they're shoveling smells more like shit

Where everybody is dirty, and everyone looks clean
I'll just keep row, row, rowing on down the stream

Gone Fishin'

I find that you can learn a lot about a person by their fishing habits. There are really only two different types of fisherman out there. It really comes down to quality versus quantity. Would you rather catch 50 sunnies or one Palomino trout?

Sunnies are easy to catch. If you go to any pond you can catch sunnies with minimum effort or time. It is usually a sure bet. A palomino on the other hand is a rare trout. They are hard to find. Even if you know where there is one, you may not be able to catch it. Even if you have the right bait, you may spend a whole day with your pole in your hand and catch nothing.

You have to know what you're after, and use the right bait. The more attractive your bait, the more fish you will attract. Be careful. As soon as your line hits the water the sunnies will be after it. There are some pretty sunnies out there. Sometimes you can't tell.

A lot of my friends when asked which they would prefer take the 50 sunnies. They feel it is better to catch more fish. It makes them feel like a more accomplished fisherman to talk about the multitudes of sunnies they have landed. When you're fishing for the palomino most of your stories are about "the one that got away". I go for the palomino every time.

The people who go for the sunnies are usually the people who hook up with someone new every time they go out. I have no problem with that, to each his own. A lot of my friends are that way. Always talking about the number of times they have scored with various women. When I see their conquests I am not surprised at all. Anybody could have caught those sunnies. In fact I spend a fair amount of my fishing time, trying to avoid those sunnies that they are so proud to catch.

I would rather talk to a beautiful girl (palomino) all night and go home alone. Palomino's are hard to catch. They are even tougher to keep hooked. I don't have to catch 50 sunnies to know that I'm an exceptional fisherman. My bait works better than most of the other fisherman I see out there. I get bites every time I go out.

I ask the trout/sunny question to people all the time. My favorite answer was when I asked this kid Zack that I met in the mountains. ("Picture this") I'm sitting at this table, having a drink in a run down mountain tavern with my buddy Danny. This kid would not shut up about the girls on the dance floor. What he would do to them, what a great dancer he was. I'm just sitting there listening to this kid run his mouth as I sip my drink and scan the room again. You know the type, talks like he's John Travolta while he's sitting on his ass, bitching at me for being a wallflower. I asked him if he ever goes fishing. He said yes, all the time. So I asked him which he would rather catch. I was curious which he would choose, the 50 sunnies or the one palomino. His answer was so absolutely perfect I have to share it with you... "Sunnies man! They taste good! I like the fat ones, because they have more meat on them!" I was grinning from ear to ear and this guy had no idea what I was even talking about. That happens a lot.

Kiss and Tell

In the back seat of the car
Outside of the bar
That was my favorite, my favorite by far

Still...I felt like a kid in a candy store
When I walked inside and shut the dressing room door
With everyone else outside
That was a good time
A personal favorite, a favorite of mine

A twisting back road
I couldn't see to drive
You just smiled and leaned to the side
That was another favorite, and a really good time!

It's great to be dirty
While you're getting clean
The shower! The shower!
Now, that's the favorite for me!

We never got a chance to fly on that plane
But I guess I really couldn't complain

...It was more than that; there was a lot of that. Honey would you disagree? It was more than that. Was it mostly that? Baby I still see you in my dreams.

Grace

Rich boys are hippies
Poor boys are gypsies
There's a cross at the bottom of the rabbit's hole
I'm not gonna tell you how I know

Losers believe in luck, winners believe in fate
The one, who has the strongest back, carries all the weight

Don't step up to me, and start throwing stones
I'll reach inside you and grab some of my own
Sling 'em from my wrist; and I don't ever miss
Take aim and hit you dead between the eyes

Quarters, pennies, nickels, and dimes
Got me a pack of cigarettes and 50 more miles

When I'm running on fumes
About to break down
I stumble to one knee
She brings it back around

Thinking back to Sunday mornings
When I was just a kid
Something about a man named Job
Faith's what I got out of it

Your seeds for tomorrow
Were planted yesterday
If you want a ticket for the show
You'll have to talk to Grace

Us/Them - The Riddle

    An undefined enemy of
dreamers, since the days of Galileo.
They or them as they are sometimes called
are the byproducts of the emptiness that we
carry within ourselves. Do I think that
there is a Doctor Evil sitting in some bunker
plotting his next attempt at global domination?
No. But I do believe that within each of us
lie two separate paths that we all must choose
from. Would you be Jesus or Emperor? What
I'm trying to say is that if you thirst for
power with an unquenchable need,
disregarding the mountains of collateral
damage that are created by your darker half. Then you have crossed
a line. You stand with them. This is not some kind of "Hippie"
propaganda that I'm trying to spread here. I'm not going and
standing outside of any building marching and bitching about some
unclear, distorted gripe that I have used to excuse my failures in life.
I am trying to give an answer to a question that was asked when
Cain killed Able.

    There are pinnacle choices that we make at random
moments throughout our lives. These choices add up to determine
the human being that we become. Within these moments there is
an internal struggle. The outcome of which is ultimately decided by
you. Good and evil are two very slippery creatures to corner and
define. Just as they and them are impossible to define. However, if
you do subscribe to the idea that there are both good and evil things
that take place in this world, you should have no problem
conceding that they are out there.

    It really is *Us and Them*, and you can't say you were never
told. You may have chosen to ignore it, or shrug it away, but this
one message has come up over and over again throughout all of our
lives. Usually on a subliminal level, in music, in your day to day, the

people you choose as friends, the places you choose to go. We don't associate with them, and they don't want to associate with Us. Sure they use Us when it benefits them, just as we use them to benefit Us. In the end you are who you run with.

"What is love anyway? Is it in the room, sitting in the corner? Point it out to me. How about forever, how long is that? Take this pen and write down the number of years that represents. You're a fool and a dreamer, and there is no place for that in these modern times".

- Sam Ohtgnitbuod, 1871

Just because something cannot be defined
...Does not mean that it isn't real.

Caught in a Web

There once was a group of young flies, which all hatched at the same time. Wiggling out of their little liquid shells, they developed wings quickly. Before you knew it they had learned to fly. Now a fly's life is very short, but these young flies were to busy discovering the world around them to question their mortality. There were 10 of these flies in particular who set out away from the rest to "discover the world around them". They were all flying through the air twisting this way and that. When suddenly they got tangled up in a web.

None of them had any idea what it was. They were young and had never encountered such a thing. Suddenly from out of nowhere a giant spider showed up and grabbed a hold of one of the flies. As the other flies watched in horror the spider wrapped his arms around the fly and sucked the life out of it. Then he just disappeared as quietly as he had arrived. The other nine flies were devastated. They had no idea what had happened to their friend. They had very limited life experience, and had never seen a spider before.

But time washes everything away and eventually it was back to business as usual. Of course there was a new element added to there existence, but for the most part they were unchanged (or at least it seemed that way). Although they were stuck in something that they didn't understand, and couldn't escape from, there were still a lot of things to discover.

One fly however had changed, even if he didn't know it. His name was Dirk. After the spider had left, it was Dirk who got everybody talking again. Just spouting out whatever he could think of to say, so that they could get past this horror and move on with their lives. His brother Vern took it the worst. Always nervous that something was going to happen, maybe that thing would come back for him. The rest of the flies were all busy dancing and frolicking as young flies do.

More time passed and eventually the spider was just a distant bad dream. Until one day when they were all watching a butterfly glide by the web, the spider returned. He appeared out of nowhere again, and grabbed a hold of Mark. Mark was the biggest fly of them all. None of the other flies were as strong as him. But, the spider took him away with the stealth of a humming bird. Leaving no trace as he disappeared out of view.

Again, Dirk calmed down all of the other flies. This time however Vern wasn't the only one who was worried. Two of the other flies, Todd and Jack began to thrash around in a panic trying to free themselves from this thing in which they found themselves caught up in. The other four flies were busy watching an Eagle in the next tree tending her eggs.

Time past by as it always does. With each passing day Todd and Jack grew more frantic. Both Dirk and Vern tried to calm them down but there was nothing they could do. Then one morning when they woke up Jack and Todd were gone. Vern began to shout "It took them, that thing came and took them!" Dirk told everyone "calm down, they must have gotten free". After that everyone calmed down. Vern sat down and twiddled his thumbs looking this way and that with nervous glances. Meanwhile Cindy and Michael were busy flirting, while Dirk played cards with John and Steph.

Then one day the spider returned again. This time he grabbed Cindy, right out of Michael's arms. Vern was yelling and beating his fists against the web. Dirk tried to reason with the spider. Michael just screamed at the top of his lungs. The spider was oblivious to any of their pleading, and simply carried Cindy away.

The day after when they all awoke Michael wouldn't wake up. They had no idea what had happened. He just went to sleep and never got up. They just figured he needed to rest after what had happened to Cindy. Dirk was counseling Vern as Steph and John counted the drops of rain. After getting Vern calmed down, he went over to check on Michael, but he was nowhere to be found. Out of the corner of his eye he thought he saw that thing carrying

Michael away but said nothing about it to the others. Instead he told them Michael must have woken up and somehow gotten away. "He's probably with Jack and Todd buzzing around somewhere". Vern looked up from the corner. He gave him a crazed, disbelieving stare and went back to ripping his hair out of his head.

A few days past and the four of them were talking about when they first flew away from home. When suddenly they saw the spider approaching again. They all began to scream and tried with all their might to get free of the web. John turned to Steph and said "I'm sorry I never told you how I really feel, but I love you". They hugged each other and prepared to embrace their fate together. Meanwhile Vern was kicking and screaming, and Dirk just stood there in silence. Thinking of the friends he had lost to this thing with no name. The spider approached just as he always did dropping down from the sky. He started to approach Steph and John, when Dirk screamed out as loud as he could. "Take me you bastard, I'm not afraid of you, leave them alone!" The spider put Steph down and turned toward Dirk. Dirk just stood there, unwilling to give this "thing" the satisfaction of his cries. When out of nowhere a giant hand came sweeping down through the web. Tearing them free as it ripped through the surface of their prison.

As the four of them were flying away Dirk glanced back to see the hand come down on top of the spider and crush it. Then he heard a voice that belonged to this new giant creature that had freed them say "I fucking hate spiders!" Then the giant thing just walked away.

...So whatever happened to the four flies who escaped the web? They went on to live out the remainder of their short lives with a new respect for life. After facing that monster that Dirk had named death. Oh yeah, and of course they all lived happily ever after.

How About a Little Sympathy

I'm not the same beast I was when I hit the ground. That was so long ago. Yes, I did think that I knew better than them. I guess I still do think that way. There's really no sense lying about that. In fact I hardly ever lie at all. It's a waste of time. If I have to be your scapegoat, I may as well use it to my benefit when possible. Especially since I am usually right. When I'm wrong I admit it. It just so happens that the few times I was wrong, cost me dearly. I know that I still intrigue you as much as I ever did. Even though you stupid humans sometimes push me to my limits.

As I look around me there are swine breeding swine at record speeds. I close my eyes in horror at your awful sense of style. Most of you don't even recognize me when we meet, which is somehow insulting. Sure, I still play around with your emotions here and there, but I'm out of the temptation racket. You guys have that covered without my help. I have to admit though; I don't detest you as much as I once did. There was a time not so long ago when I was disgusted with your ignorance. The things that you covet sicken me, especially the gluttons and the sloth's. I would ask myself how I could be cast down so low, while you idiots prosper. Now I just laugh.

I am amused with your mundane repetition, and lack of meaning. It just proves how special I am. Yes I've changed a lot over the years. I have to admit, I still haven't quite gotten over my preoccupation with the pleasures of the flesh. I try to avoid confrontation whenever I can, but I look forward to the next time I get cornered. You don't need me to be the bad guy anymore. You people do things to one another that I could have never thought up. In fact, I think I'm going to take a vacation. Maybe I'll go hang out in Tibet and do a little meditating. Actually, that's not my scene. I'll most likely try on some new faces, and see how they fit, mingle a little with the locals. OK I gotta go, I have some quick business to take care of down south.

Remember I never pulled a trigger. I only tempt the finger. Who has sent more people running to the open arms of the Church than I?

Home Sweet Home

So the birds are finally back. I saw a Robin the other day. Thank God. I made it through another winter. I'm sure that when I die it will be in the winter. Every year it takes a little more away. Maybe that's why all the old folks head for Florida? I'm so happy to see those birds, but it makes me feel a little guilty. I used to shoot so many birds when I was younger. For no real reason at all. Just for the "fun" of it. BB gun, .22, shotgun, when you grow up in the country there's a lot of time to kill. I used up a fair part of mine killing various little animals I encountered with my pals in the woods around town. Fishing and causing mischief were also two of my other favorite past times. I never really took into account that these birds were living things. They were just birds. Now I can't wait to see them at the beginning of spring.

I knew even less about life and death back then, then I do now. Ever since I was in elementary school, I thought I would be dead by 25. I guess everybody thinks that. When you're young you can't imagine being "old". The thing that fascinates me about this, is that in a way I did. I'm not the same person I was. It was like I woke up one day and everything was different, but it was still the same to everybody else around me. I shed my skin, or I moved in, I'm not sure which.

One way to describe it is to imagine an empty house on a hill. The house represents your body. It's just a skeletal frame with some wiring. Without a spirit, or a "spark", it's just a box. This house is a rental. Throughout its life different people live within its walls. Since its a rental nobody can stay there forever. When people leave a house they always leave something behind - a photo album, a hole in the wall, or a plate of brownies for the new tenant. Sometimes the house is a mess when you move in and you have to fix it up. That's how my house was when I moved in. So you pick up the photo album and check it out. It tells you a little about the person who lived here before "you".

Our lives are very similar. We have boxes of old memories sitting on the shelves in our subconscious. Just like a photo album left behind by a stranger. You look through it and very few things are clearly remembered. When your parents tell you the story that goes with the picture your mind shows you what you think you remember. The chances are that "you" were not there at all. The few memories you have are from that photo album you found when you moved in. The spare baggage left behind by the last tenant. Did they leave it there on purpose? Were they in a hurry to get out?

Sometimes your lease expires and you just don't have time to gather up all of your things. However they got there, they're your memories now, your photo album to page through. There are quite a few photos in my basement. I even have some video.

...Just like the seasons change, so do we.

Walking around back home
I see memories everywhere
I might take a glance
I don't stop to stare
The past is gone
Right or wrong
I just shrug my shoulders
And move along

The Pit

It was she I followed to the Pit
It was me I found inside of it
He told me stories from the past
How the true winner will finish last

Friends in time will turn away
I, he said am here to stay
Just a shadow of the son
The rest of him is gone

Take my hand
Walk through the clouds
Most of them will be gone
Before you come back down

The music has never been the same
He wears my face and shoulders my pain
Talk to him in the mirror
The words he says grow clearer everyday

I would love to know who decided that fuck is a bad word. It's my favorite word. In fact, "fuck-it" is my mantra. Whenever I get stressed out, or I'm feeling down. I just touch my thumb to my finger and repeat the phrase until I'm calm again (try it, it works every time). What other word has so much feeling behind it? It is so versatile, and direct. It's like putting an explanation point at the end of a sentence. The only other word that comes close to it is cool. After all it's only a word. Lighten' the fuck up!

Listen, I'm no military genius, or a government scholar of any kind but I hear there are rules in war. I was listening to a Warren Haynes cover my friend gave me. He was singing that Dylan song "blowin' in the wind". The line that popped out was the one about cannon balls, how long until they're forever banned. I heard somewhere that there is a group of nations who decided that they should ban and remove all land mines. Obviously these fucking things should have never been planted to begin with, but that's not what puzzles me the most. What is being said here is...when we kill each other, land mines are against the rules. There are rules?!

We (the human species) have been at war for so long we have actually developed rules? What is this? Is it just a game? Are landmines the same thing as holding a receiver? Is this just a business with a handbook? "How to kill the enemy, the right way" Killing is in our nature, we are animals after all. Animals kill to eat, to protect their territory, and if need be, to maintain their dominant status against challengers. They do it face to face, which instantly changes the psychology of any struggle. This also means that they risk their life in the process. There is something fair and true in that. Breaking even. We have deviated from that natural way of doing things.

So isn't it odd that the leaders (who never risk their lives in combat) of our countries visit foreign countries and meet with other leaders. They don't attack each other when they meet. Why is that? If there is such a difference between us and them why doesn't your instinct take over and kill the threat. Is it because they can send someone else to do it for them?

They sit there like two coaches before a game discussing rules. What is going on? How can you make rules? War is about death. It's ok to shoot someone with a 50 cal. off a helicopter, but landmines are wrong? There is no logic in that. Nothing natural. It is the ass backwards logic of human beings. They can agree that neither side wants to get blown up by landmines. Hopefully one day they will rethink that bullets thing too.

The Twins

I'm on the edge of the storm
So forgive me if I fall
I put the numbers down on paper
They add up to nothing at all

There's a puzzle on the table, I have to admit
There were a few wrong pieces, I tried to make fit

There's a pounding in my chest

I was running down the trail
The reeds brushed against my face
When I finally turned around
 I had lost my place

There's a knocking at the door

Do you want some more?
I have so much to give
Do you want to hear the answers?
They are mine alone to give

I shut the door behind me
Standing with the twins
One said call me He
My brother's name is Him

There's a ringing in my ears

Kindness of a Stranger

6-10-05

The other night I was all stressed out, and beating myself up about having to "get out there". You know, not wait for anybody else and just go to the bars alone. I do it fairly regularly now. I look at it like it's conditioning. Building the perfect beast and all that. I'm not even a big drinker. I just can't sit at home, besides Stargate was a rerun.

Anyway I end up going to this bar for a drink. There was a $4 cover because they had a band there. So I go sit at the bar. I ran through 5 cigarettes, and one drink in record time. There were no girls there that caught my eye, and I usually try to avoid people who know my face. It felt like an eternity there on the barstool, but it was probably 20-30 minutes.

So I get up to leave, as I walk out the door the bouncer gives me a weird look (I get that all the time) and says goodnight. Then as I was walking to my truck in the parking lot he comes out and stops me. I'm thinking "ok, now what did I do". He hands me back my four bucks and asks what happened. He meant, what makes you spend four dollars to sit at a bar for twenty minutes. He was sincere; he actually wondered what makes a guy like me come out to a bar alone at 11o'clock at night to pay a cover for one drink. I spared him the drama and said I just wanted a drink. He shook my hand and said, "Hey, take care brother!" That meant more to me than anything else I can think of in a long time. The kindness of a random stranger.

The Big Game...

So the day is finally here

Where are you gonna be in the big game

There are a lot of has-been benchwarmers out there

Looking over their shoulders at their best days

A lot that were last to be picked in the minors

Are out front in the big game

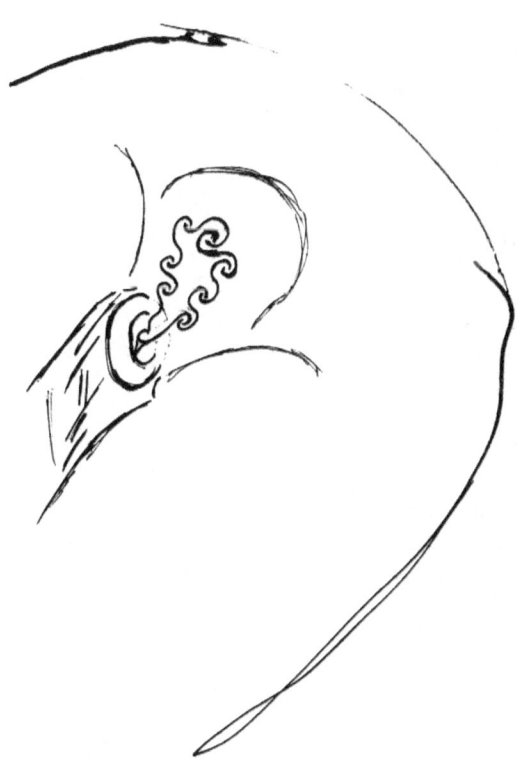

Skeleton Key

I'm here now
I wasn't here then
Before too long
I won't be here again

I talk too fast
The wheels turn slow
It was an uphill climb
Baby, I know, I know

Now you say you're out of pity
Honey ain't it a shame
Used up all your cards
For one more hand in the game

You found it in the dark
Trying to bring it to the light
Can split a man in two
It'll be alright

It's an uphill climb
Baby, I know, I know
You talk too fast
The wheels turn slow

If you give me a chance
I'll show you a dream
Open up the doors
With my skeleton key

So you feel something very strongly, and you feel compelled to tell everyone. There are varying opinions on the subject. You get frustrated because you think nobody is listening. You start to scream and they start to scream and nobody hears anyone. You may as well whisper it. The same people will hear you.

There are numerous different personalities, and people to go with them. To me, there are really only two different types of people. My people, and the others. Either you understand me and the things I say, or you don't. My words make you feel, or they make no sense at all. I like it that way. After all I'm not your father or a preacher. I might be a teacher? I'm not sure. When I hear that McCartney song "band on the run", it always makes me smile. That's who we are, the band on the run. You can't catch us because we move on the wind. Drifting in and out of your consciousness like water through the cracks of a wall. You know when I am with you because the world opens up. Once you know me, you can never turn your back away. You can only deny me. In doing so you only deny yourself. Blanketing yourself in false truths and alibis, you deny your senses. Lost, you only achieve a small percentage of your true self.

...If anything is possible, everything is

Saying something brings it one step closer to life.

Stop

When I was younger I lived in a small town. Actually it is a village. My parents always told us not to go past the stop sign. This stop sign represented my border when I was growing up. Within the safety of my street nothing could hurt me. However if I were to wander past the stop sign any number of bad things would happen. I'm sure that my mom just had bad things happen to her, and she wanted to protect us.

Almost as soon as the boundary was set, I began to go past it. Just a little at first, looking down the road to make sure I didn't get caught. Then just blowing right past, and not even looking back. It's funny how often I think about that stop sign, and what it represented in my life. We moved out of the house I grew up in. Thankfully my parents still live in the same town. I have to be honest; there is always a feeling of safety when I enter my town. I'm glad that stop sign was there. I'm glad it's still there today. When I grew up I learned outside of my town, there are no boundaries. Every time I have to put one up, I see that dented old stop sign.

We've all been screwed over and we've all fucked up. At a point there comes a time when you say enough is enough. You shoulder all the weight. You question and you debate. With your two feet you make a stand. Then you are a man.

Guessing Game

Let's play the guessing game _ _ _ _ _ _ _ _

I'm thinking of a thing that's 8 letters long

It means absolutely nothing, but it means everything

If you haven't ever been there, you haven't a clue

A wild free for all, freak petting zoo

Once a year down Tennessee way

Water spouting magic mushroom, complete with light display

Bobble heads on sticks, lot's of music too

Is any of this sounding familiar to you

If you're a little crazy, nobody can tell

Take a look around, they're all crazy as well

Old school and new school, everybody learns something here

Wash down that hangover with a nice cold beer

Wave goodbye to the moon with bloodshot eyes

Try to fall asleep before the sun can rise

Listen very closely I've been around a time or two

You better get some shut eye before the heat gets to you

Because the sun will rise, sad but true

Once the heat rolls in there will be no sleeping for you

Dad's Hands

There is never enough time to spend with the ones we love. Time is moving faster every day. Most things seem the same. We look at ourselves and the changes are so small that we miss them. The one place that I can see the passing of time is in my father's hands.

I remember when I was little and my dad would take me to my Grandfathers to help him clean up the yard. We would pick up branches, and burn brush. My father, just like his father before him had working mans hands. They were ruff and they were strong. My Grandfathers hands were also strong, they had sunspots all over them from a life spent working outside. My father's hands had no spots and seemed huge compared to mine.

Over time even as a child I noticed my Grandfathers hands slowly turn to that silky see through skin that old people get. I didn't notice my father's hands changing until a few years ago. I had noticed that my hands had become ruff and strong like my fathers were, but in my twenties dads hands were still pretty much the same.

I guess I was about 30 when I noticed the sunspots starting to appear on my dad's hands. I'm not really sure what to say about it. Time wouldn't listen even if I had a great argument to present him with. I guess it is just a thing that I noticed is all.

Monster and the Martyr

There's a Monster and a Martyr and they live inside of me
Which one I choose to listen to, changes constantly
Maybe I'll help a drowning man
Maybe I'll watch him float down stream
There's a Monster and a Martyr, and they live inside of me

I may hold your hand, or push you away
It all depends on the moment, and it changes constantly
If one kind word is all you really need to hear
I may creep up behind you and whisper it in your ear
I may cut you with my tongue and bring you to your knees
There's a Monster and a Martyr inside of me who do just as they please

My Monster may suffer from vanity, but my Martyr he takes the blame
I take counsel from both sides, and I love/fear them both the same
One tells me I'm enlightened, the other one says I'm insane
One tries to fill my glass, the other pours it down the drain
There's a Monster and a Martyr inside of me, they do just as they please
However, I'm the one who chooses, what I decide to be

Everything has been said but not everyone has said it..

- Morris King "Mo" Udall

I wish I could find a cool way to summarize this book. Some deep intellectual shit! Tell you what it is and what it represents. Sum my life up in a play on words. Honestly, though, after thinking of nothing to say I decided just to be honest. I have no idea. I bashed my head against the wall until it cracked, and this is the shit that fell out. Just an abstract slice of the whole. Some of the things in this book were written years ago and some a few weeks ago. I'm not represented by any one thought in these pages. They are moments in my life where I felt something. If you're still here there had to be at least one thing you could relate to. If not, you must be sitting the bench (which is your choice to make).

Some of the places that I've been when I wrote this stuff, I will never go back to again. Other places I've been, I hope to see again one day. However the majority of these were written in a place I never leave. So it is what it is. Whatever that is? I hope you get something out of it. Whether the cover catches your eye or you just stop and say "hi". Either way if you are interested in some way and you took the time to try and understand, thank you I appreciate it, hopefully I made it worth your Time.

8-21-06

Tourist

Life is a vacation. You leave the core for a short time and enter the physical. There are many people who use their vacation to be tourists. They go to the same places and get their post cards, and T-shirts. This is the same way they live their lives. They never really take the time to look around. Choosing instead to spend their time collecting "crap".

Over the years more and more shit accumulates. You don't throw anything away. You have the fancy china locked away in a cabinet. You're eating off of plastic plates. Why? Why not use the china, or throw it away. Because you have trained yourself to believe that the china represents a moment in your life. In actuality it is just another gift you are wasting. It just takes up space, another nick-knack on a shelf. Something else to dust and worship as if it holds some value in your "life".

You have Star Wars on VHS, DVD, and soon on Blu Ray. What is all of this shit for? I think that many people need these things so they have "something to show for it". My advice is to invite some friends over and eat cheeseburgers off of that china. You may as well live your life. Spend your time and money going out and living in the moment. The life of a tourist always ends the same. Your stuff is auctioned off to the highest bidder. One day someone's dog will be eating out of the dish that was too nice for you to ruin.

Yeah, life is a big beautiful fucking mess. You sit back from a distance and watch. Masturbating your dreams, only to come up with a flaccid response. It's in sight, and it looks good. You can almost touch it. Then it's over. Blue balls and pipe dreams, a list of hits and misses. You work up a sweat, and then hold back. You try to make it last, dancing on the tip of a needle. A few shakes and shivers and the feeling is gone. Before you know it, it's over.

Why do it today?
Put it off until tomorrow
You spend your life in despair and sorrow
You're the one to blame
Sloth is your name

Don't go outside, it's safer in here
Shovel down your meal
Drink another beer
The hardest button to button
Larger than life...the Glutton

No Alibis

Obviously the goal is to overcome our fears and insecurities. Everyone has something. It may be childhood baggage, or the loss of something close to you. You have to confront and deal with these issues. The only other choice is to admit defeat. If you don't try you will never know.

I see allot of people who have just given up. Every obstacle is another excuse to do nothing. Don't get me wrong; I've done my fair share of pouting in the past. I think it lessened me as a person. Life is not for the weak. If you're not able to stand on your own, you will fall. That's when you see what you're made of.

There is no such thing as attempted suicide, only people grasping at straws, and begging for help and attention. If you want out, put a twelve gauge in your mouth. That will most certainly get the job done. Pathetic I tell ya! You sloth your life away hoping for someone to save you. Why would anyone save you if you don't even try to save yourself? There are plenty of people out there in worse situations than you, trying as hard as they can to stay alive. You are slowly killing yourself everyday. Crying and whining like a baby. Guess what? Mommy can't fix it. Chances are she's fucked up too.

Nobody has an answer to your problem. It's your problem. We all have our own.

Go to the mirror and stare into it for 3 minutes. Are you happy with what you see? What has this person done with the time they have been given? Would you do the same if it were "you"? Is it someone you would want to know? If your answer is no, you have some work to do. The other option is to ignore it and take it out on everyone and everything around you until you are alone. This brings you back to the mirror again. You can only run so far, eventually you will have to face the face. The longer you wait, the more time you waste. In the end you are a murderer if you do nothing. You end up torturing that helpless victim in the mirror for its whole life.

Why is this so? Maybe its faith, or the lack thereof? Somewhere along the way we all lose faith. If this is the case, who am I to judge? How do I convince you there is something worth believing in? Can I tell you about the right song or a smile from a stranger at just the right time? That smell in the spring. How do I show you the thoughts it reveals? The mixing of memory and senses that react like electricity running through me. The first time I was listening just the right way and I could hear the woods talking to me. The crinkling of dead leaves or bending of a tree limb telling you a squirrel is nearby.

The way that with the right set of eyes you can see how it comes together, but can never really put it into words. If you look there are always signs. If you don't look, they were never there at all. It was just the wind whispering its song. Like I said faith is something that can't be explained. So I won't bother even trying to tell you.

Mystery Man

He worships the son
The sun gives him a tan
The mystery man, the mystery man

With a Grin on his face
A stiff drink in his hand
The mystery man, the mystery man

They don't know where he comes from
They don't care were he's been
It's never enough; it's always too much
Go on and shake his hand

I remembered how I met him
Though I forget where and when
The mystery man, the mystery man

I'd love to tell you his secret
One day you'll understand
Until that time comes back around
It has to stay a mystery man

Title Goes Here

I was doing my time, in the belly of a whale

When a Siamese cat grabbed me by the tail

He told me a secret out there on the sea

Something about him was familiar to me

It's the same old story as it's always been

One walks out as another walks in

Did you pass yourself walking through the door?

Now I'm running round in circles

Casting seeds wherever I go

But do they grow, do they grow

So very slow, very slow

It's the human condition; I've got it for sure

Every time I get what I want, I want more

All the good guys are bad, the bad ones are good

We don't know the answer why, maybe we should

I've spent all this time trying to figure it out. It's still a puzzle to me. Every door opened reveals two more. The time I have spent chasing the Phoenix. Years. Endless. The things I have laid on the alter. Friends, loves, and still it is out of my reach. In your time and space, can you say you have done the same? Can I say you should? This book is a drop in a cup that is overflowing.

Now, with my twenties behind me, who can say what's ahead of me? Most people spend their lives in the dark. I have seen the light, and embraced it, only to realize the hopeful hopelessness of it all. There is no golden ticket in my mailbox, but I still check it everyday. Trying to stay afloat and not get pulled under by the traps that "game reality" sets for us at every turn.

So I no longer think I will change the world with a clever rhyme, or parable that will make everyone stop and listen. I'm not waiting for a big bang to mix it all up. Instead I make small advances in my everyday life.

Picture this...there is a big quarry lake. One side of the lake is faced with a sheer slate wall towering 150 feet above the water. The other sides are grass and dirt covered shoreline. A piece of the Cliffside breaks off and crashes into the water, creating a wave. This wave turns into a ripple. The ripple pushes a branch to the shore. A caterpillar climbs off the branch to the safe ground it has washed up on. It climbs a tree and builds a cocoon. You know the rest. None of that would have been possible if the rock hadn't hit the water. The caterpillar would be fish food. Everything affects everything. I affect everyone that I crash into in this crazy, crazy world. So do you.

The Answer

Off in the distance you see the answer

You already know the answer

You don't want to know the answer

You go in search of the answer

When you get close enough, you remember

You turn and run from the answer

There is a peace that washes over you

You feel nervous, like you have forgotten something

Off in the distance you see the answer

You already know the answer

You don't want to know the answer

You go in search of the answer

Art

Art is a slippery son of a bitch, but you gotta love him. Most of the time he is misunderstood. He can be interpreted in many different ways. Nobody really knows what he is up to. If you want to understand him you will. He is a child. He can be hateful, and selfish. He is filled with never-ending wonder of everything around him. He's the mystery man. He can turn a lump of coal into a crazy diamond. He is a name and a thing. He can make you dance and he can make you sing. He takes everything.

What to Wear?

Clyde is a peculiar fellow
Who thinks too much to be mellow
One sunny day he decided to go into town

His closet was empty and bare
Only two shirts hung there
The decision to choose
Became that of the ethical kind

One shirt was white the other one black
He wished there was a grey shirt hanging on the rack

The white looks neat, and makes him feel good
But keeping it clean takes more than it should
The black shirt is cool, but it draws the heat
Makes him look shady to the people he meets

Grey would be much better
At least it seems that way to Clyde
This black and white thing is just another worry on his mind

Medium Rare

As she stood there preaching to me, I couldn't help wondering what vegetarian tastes like. They always eat good food, they're fairly healthy, I'll bet she goes running every morning. She looked pretty damn healthy to me. Looking at her nice tan thighs I can imagine myself just taking a bite. Then I realize I'm drifting off on one of my little daydreams. So with all my might I try to pay attention to what she is saying.

"...I'm just saying you really shouldn't eat meat, you should be a vegetarian it's better for you. Eating flesh is so barbaric".

I'm sure someone has said this to you at some point in your life. We all know somebody who is either a full fledge vegetarian, a faux vegetarian, or God bless their hearts an honest to goodness vegan. Ya' know what? I really don't have a problem with that...whatever floats your boat kid. However, when they start to preach enlightenment while lacking a basic understanding of life, I get a bit irritated.

Here's the kicker boys and girls...life costs life. In order to stay alive we must all take life from something else. Plants are alive because they take life from the nutrients in the ground. If you eat a plant, you are a killer...just like the rest of us. The fact that you exist at all is proof you have taken life. It's a big fucking circle, and you are part of it.

Everything is alive, and the spirit moves in all things. So don't go getting all high and mighty and think that you are somehow a better human being because you don't eat meat. You take something else's life in order to sustain your own. Just because it doesn't cry doesn't mean it isn't alive. Did you ever think about that?

Fear Seed

When the path came upon yet another forest, I asked Art where we were going. He said, "This is the wilderness. The seeds of fear that you have allowed to take root have become the forest you see before you. Look upon the fears of your youth that are now blocking the sun.

Though you may chop a few down, there are always new seeds taking root in your soul. Your task is not to cut down every tree. That is a task no man can accomplish. Besides it is right for a man to have some fear, but you must find your path. Be careful not to lose your way. No one can tell you where your path begins and ends. It is something you must find on your own".

He handed me an axe and disappeared as silently as he appeared. I looked out at the forest before me. I could hear a whispering in the wind. The more I listened the more I understood. I walked into the forest with my axe in hand. I could hear the trees mocking me. The Redwood high in the clouds looking down on me "Look how small you are. You little bastard! Look what you got yourself into this time. I always knew you were no good. Bastards go to hell! If you're born in sin, you can never win! "

The little apple tree snickered "Are you happy now? Where is your son? I don't see him anywhere. What was his name again? Cross was it? You have no wife. You blew it! She had your baby with someone else. You have squandered your days drinking rum and pursuing pleasure".

The forest was endless and the voices were many. A sadistic teacher from school in the shape of a willow. A thorn tree with the voice of an estranged friend. It became too much to bare.

I decided to sit down and talk it over with my shadow. Something of this magnitude must be agreed upon by both of us. His eyes were wild and filled with rage. His empty stare changed into a sinister grin as he said, "Let's burn the whole fucking thing down! Who the hell do these trees think they are? I'm not going down like this!" I replied "I know your upset, but if we start this place on fire we may not get out of here alive. Here's the plan. I take this axe that Art gave us and we cut that fucking Redwood down. It will take out quite a few of the trees around it. Look how fucking big it is. Then when it hit's the ground we will start it on fire." He said "Let's start that fucker on fire first!" I replied, "Now you're talking.

I picked up the axe and walked over to the base of the redwood, ignoring it's taunts and threats I swung the axe with all my might. A black liquid began to pour out of the gash I had made. The tree began to scream and I wailed at it over and over again until the screams turned to a dull whimper. Then all of the other trees began to scream and threaten me. I struck the final blow and the Redwood let out a final splintering cry as it fell to the ground. Then my shadow said "I thought we were gonna start it on fire first" to which I replied "sorry, I forgot. You can burn it now". He was laughing as he walked the length of the redwood starting little brush fires as I turned my attention to some of the other trees.

We went on like this for what seemed like years. Time does not work the same on the crooked path. The two of us cleared out a trail through the trees. After getting through the forest I reached a clearing where I used some of the trees to make a cabin. I lived there alone for a time. Until one day there was a knock on the door. I knew who it was before I opened the door.

I let Art in and I grabbed the bottle of rum from my shelf. We sat down at the table. "You have done well for yourself. You faced your fears and made a home out of what you could salvage. You have kept yourself warm on the long cold nights with only your shadow to keep you company. You have taken that which was ugly and mean and tamed it with your will. The one I serve is very pleased. As reward for this task I have been instructed to give you more time. Your lust for life will sustain you while others wither at the vine. Now it is time that we go. I still have many wonders to show you". I walked over to my dresser and put on my necklace, and rings. I sat down and pulled up my boots, grabbed my jacket and stepped out the door. I gave one last look at what will soon be my past as I gazed once more upon my crooked path.

Golden Ticket

Willie, Willie, you're so silly
I hope you got a ticket for me
Cause' I've been good and done what I should
You know that I believe
Oh Alice, Alice wont you tell me how you got away

Run! Run! She said you better get away
But I can't leave the rest of you here feeling this way
It isn't always bad
In fact it's mostly good
Fix a couple little things we always knew we should

I always liked it when the good guys worked with the bad
To get rid of the evil things that make us all so sad
But while black and white are fighting
The gray begins to grow
Explosions are enlightening all the seeds that we have sewn

But hey I'm just a singer and this is just a song
Nothing is between us but the lines that they have drawn
Come on take my hand we'll make it if we try
What you gonna do boy just sit there and cry
We'll dream a little daydream or listen to a song
Swallow up your pride my friend and admit you're sometimes wrong

Ringo said it don't come easy
Yes sir that's a fact
So we better move ahead instead of looking back
There ain't no future in the past the best that I can tell

This fleeting moment has past us by and now I too must go
Hope I turned you on to some things that you didn't know
It all comes down to right and wrong
And only time will tell
Think on this a little more...I bid you all farewell

Balloon

Remember when we were little? We would go outside with a balloon and tie on that note. You stand there and watch it float away, wondering how far it will go. This book is my balloon, my message in a bottle. I can't help but wonder where it will land.

The greatest and most important problems of life are all fundamentally insoluble. They can never be solved, only outgrown.

- Carl Gustav Jung

~ On Bended Knee ~

If the world is one big stage. I would like to thank the following characters for playing their pivotal roles in my story. You were all cast perfectly.

...Mom, Dad, Leon, Vera, Odin, Merlin, Justice, Oz.-Lex.-Giz., Bleise, Holly, Seth, Jen B., my Truck, Jeremy (S.D.), Gene, Kristen, Brad, Erinn, Nate, Amanda, Carolyn, Danny, Charlie, Linda, Darren, Neil, Sylvia, Mia, Sterling, Cliff, and of course the countless random strangers along the way.

You can contact me at:

www.JCAngst.com